The Masquerade Ball at the Lighthouse

The Sea Crest Lighthouse Series

Book 4

Carolyn Court

Kindle Create Publishing

With contributions from
Thomas A Hickok, Jr.

Carolyn
Court

Enjoy!

Manufactured in the United States of America

10 9 8 7 6 5 4 3 2 1

Dedicated to my wonderful son, Thomas A Hickok, Jr.

Tom, thanks for always sharing my adventures. You constantly come up with ways to make our time together the best.

I'm grateful for your insight into the smugglers' minds in my book's storyline. Your ideas proved to be way better and funnier. As your mom, I'm still unsure how you know this stuff, but I've decided not to probe too deeply into it and just go with it.

Thanks for happily supporting and sharing my projects, living the 'Anonymous Acts of Kindness' lifestyle, and showing your generous heart daily.

I'm the luckiest mom in the world!

Also By Carolyn Court

Fiction

The Sea Crest Lighthouse Series

The Heart of the Lightkeeper's Daughter

Book One

The Lightkeeper's Secret

Book Two

The Key to the Lighthouse Cornerstone

Book Three

Chapter One

Mary Beth froze as she stared across the floor at the masked figure who had just arrived at the Sea Crest Lighthouse Masquerade Ball! Her dance partner awkwardly stumbled and stepped on her foot.

"What's Happening?" Jeffery Williams wondered. "Excuse me," he muttered in surprise.

However, she never heard him. Mary Beth removed her hand from Jeffrey's and covered her mouth in shock! She didn't comprehend what he'd said as she thought, *"I have dreamed of this man for years. Granted, he is masked, but so is the man of my dreams. The star of the two 'Zorro' movies!"*

She paused to catch her breath, trying to comprehend where this guy came from. *"He looks just like Antonio Banderas."*

Meanwhile, the undercover Drug Enforcement Administration (DEA) agent with the newly created identity took this all in with utter delight as he spotted her from across the room. *"She's wearing the silver flapper dress Grace told me she'd be wearing."*

As their eyes met, Antonio slowly approached the band leader. He never took his eyes off Mary Beth as he gave the man his request note, with a substantial tip, and requested, "S'il vous plaît?" (If you please?)

The band leader read the note, smiled, and said, "C'est mon plaisir!" (It's my pleasure!)

As the band began playing the theme music from The Mask of Zorro, Antonio turned and moved towards Mary Beth. He smiled when he saw her dazzling silver flapper costume. *"Wow! Now that's indescribably awesome! This is going to be fun!"* He slowly walked straight toward her, never taking his eyes off her.

Mary Beth thought, *"Wow, I must be dreaming."*

However, Jeffery wasn't feeling so dreamy as he watched this strange attraction play out. He wondered, *"Who is this guy? I will have Maggie run a check on him as soon as possible!"*

By this time, Antonio was right in front of Maggie. He offered her his hand as he thought, *"What a knockout!"*

What he actually whispered was, "Puis-je avoir cette danse?" (May I have this dance?)

All Mary Beth could utter was, "Oui," (Yes) as she took his hand.

He took her in his arms, and they danced away.

Jeffrey Williams was left standing as he wondered, *"What just happened? The nerve of that guy! He didn't even say, 'May I cut in?' and it was like Mary Beth was in a trance or something."*

Meanwhile, the masked intruder reflected on how wonderful Mary Beth felt in his arms. *"Boy, Grace told me that Mary Beth had a crush on Antonio Banderas, but she never mentioned how beautiful she was. She is so graceful; she could be a professional dancer."*

Meanwhile, Grace and Joe were pleasantly observing how their latest setup was going. They had secretly devised their usual clandestine pranks to throw Mary Beth and Antonio together. They're up to their old tricks again.

When they were asked what kind of wedding celebration they wanted when the newlyweds returned to Sea Crest, they agreed they'd like a Masquerade Ball at the lighthouse.

Grace added her wish, "We'd like to hire the same company that provided the wonderful dance floor for Kate and Michael's wedding celebration. We want the same floor design they had on the beach beneath the Sea Crest Lighthouse. Those click-together blocks that lit up the dance floor were marvelous."

Antonio was so unexpectedly drawn to Mary Beth that he started to feel strangely guilty for tricking her in this way. *"Am I imagining it, or do I detect a very faint scent of Chanel N°5? It's one of my favorite memories from my days in Paris. It makes me want to hug her closer. I'm genuinely loving this dance."*

Before this evening, he had privately been informed that she had a dramatic crush on the Zorro actor Antonio Banderas. *"Now I feel ridiculous and regret coming to this Masquerade Party disguised as the man she's attracted to. She doesn't know that I am dancing incognito. Playing a part, I performed numerous times as the stand-in and stunt-double for the real Antonio Banderas for the Zorro movies."*

Mary Beth was dancing in a dream, *"Wow! I can't fathom how this man moves perfectly with me to this theme music. We are in perfect harmony. Our natural skill level is perfectly executed, and he brings out the best in me."*

About this time, Antonio was trying to figure out how to escape this situation and save face with this beautiful creature when he thought he viewed his answer. *"I see we're headed towards the edge of the floor, lined with various potted plants and trees. It's time to make my move."*

Antonio proceeded to twirl Mary Beth around twice. He carefully remembered the dance moves from his many movie parts as he counted the beats. *"Okay, 'Open break,' as I move to separate from Mary Beth."*

As she swirled to face him, he had vanished! The expected 'Closed Break,' which should have brought the two dancers back to face each other, was gone. Mary Beth felt the silver fringe on her flapper dress fall motionless as she wondered, *"What just happened?"* She remained stock-still at the edge of the dance floor, with her arms open, ready to rejoin Zorro. However, he did not appear. *"Did I just imagine I was just twirling around with the most exciting dancer I've ever encountered?"*

Chapter Two

As Mary Beth stared blankly at the wall of potted greenery before her, a feeling of loss settled around her. *"Who was that masked man? He came directly to me like he was choosing to dance with me. The dance was wonderful. Where did he disappear to? This whole encounter feels surreal."*

The music had changed to one of her beloved tango melodies. This usually filled her with joy. This time, the familiar notes held a strange sadness that would linger for the remainder of the evening.

Jeffrey Williams slowly walked over to join her. "Wow! Who was that guy?"

Mary Beth's voice was almost a whisper as she admitted, "I don't really know. He acted like he knew me and wanted to dance with me, but I guess I was wrong."

"The nerve of that guy! If he bothers you again, I won't let anything happen to you."

"Thanks, but that won't be necessary. I don't even know who he is."

"In that case, may I have this dance?" asked Jeffrey.

As Mary Beth stepped back into his arms, he added, "By the way, I think you look terrific in that flapper costume."

"Don't get me wrong," he quickly said. "I loved the ball gown you arrived in. However, this one is much better for most dances."

"Yes, the ball gowns require excessive space, restricting the number of couples this dance floor would accommodate. I thought it was wonderful that the invitations suggested that the dress code for the ball is a 'little progressive.'"

He laughed as he recalled, "I've never seen the change of clothes explained on an invitation before. 'Please arrive in a 'ball gown' if you'd like. However, after the first couple of dances, the 'progressive dress code' will be geared toward something that requires a larger dance floor. We want everyone to be able to dance, so please bring a change into something entertaining and fun but a whole lot slimmer!"

"I know," laughed Mary Beth. "I cracked up when I read it! Leave it to Grace! She understands that many of our fellow Sea Crest Dance Studio members love dancing. We have regular classes for line dances, swing dances, and the tango.

"Our members are friendly, but many are not paired as couples. It's almost like the 'group dates' at proms nowadays; we are all welcome to come and share a good time."

"Well, just for the record, you looked perfect in your ball gown," he smiled.

"Thank you for your kind words."

She looked around and was strangely disappointed because Zorro had not resurfaced yet. She didn't want Jeffrey to notice that she was upset, so she commented, "Well, it looks like everyone is having a wonderful time."

When that musical selection ended, Joe Lawrence and his new bride, Grace, took the opportunity to make some announcements. "Hello, everyone," Joe started. "Thank you for joining us to celebrate our wedding. As most of you know, we married in Tahiti last month."

This was met with wild applause from friends and family. A couple of exuberant guests yelled, "What took you so long?" "It looks like a paradise!" "Beautiful!"

"We appreciate everyone coming. We do have another fun invitation for all of you regional history fanatics. The Sea Crest Museum committee is sponsoring a scavenger hunt with a French road-rally format. That seems like a fun way to involve the whole community plus enhance our tourism. It's also a terrific means to raise money for the project."

"Yes," added Grace. "We plan to call in favors from a couple of people, who shall remain nameless until we have surprised them with our plans."

"Well," Joe laughed. "We have high hopes of getting their cooperation without using legal persuasion. By the way, if anyone asks you for assistance with the scavenger hunt, please help out!"

Everyone laughed and clapped as they agreed.

Grace added, "It's a popular idea that could become an annual event if it proves successful."

She glanced over the crowd of well-wishers, spotted Mary Beth, and wondered, *"Now, why does she look so solemn? I think that Zorro guy dancing with her looked like a match made in heaven."*

Mary Beth hugged Grace and Joe as the celebration ended, and she said her goodbyes. "I've been so honored to be at both of your weddings in Tahiti. What an exciting tale you have to tell your grandchildren. You were married on the United States Coast Guard Cutter, which was at sea. Next, you were blessed to be married at the top of the Tahiti Lighthouse. The legacy of your ancestral connection to the great Captain James Cook was proven by the pictures in your grandmother's locket. The key to your lineage was hidden in the cornerstone of our Sea Crest Lighthouse."

Maggie stepped forward to hug the bride and groom. "Yes! Your story is one of the most memorable and exciting discoveries yet. James was sorry he missed the weddings, but he's thrilled that you two finally fell in love. He still has some pranks stored up to play on you guys. He said, 'pay-backs are never off the table where you are concerned.'"

"Hey, you two would never have gotten together if we hadn't set you up," laughed Joe! "We did you a favor!"

As they had done a million times before, Mary Beth and Maggie slipped off their shoes to walk the beach to their cars.

As Mary Beth's foot touched the cool evening sand, it felt familiar, and she loved it. She was quietly remembering the strange dance with the masked man. She was deep in thought as she whisked off her black wig and pondered, *"I don't know why he left, and I don't know who he was. Not that it matters in the least; however, I spent the rest of the night trying to discover what happened to him. But he was nowhere in sight."*

Maggie was enjoying the rhythm of the surf crashing on the shore. "I think you could keep perfect time to any music while listening to these waves. Boy, aren't we lucky? I never want to live anywhere else."

That remark reminded Mary Beth about her upcoming Real Estate assignment, so she asked Maggie, "When are we meeting to go over housing options for the new Drug Enforcement Administration Special Agents that are going to be working on the smuggling problems along the beach?"

"Sometime this coming week. One of the agents has been checking out locations along the coast that seem ideal. But we need the most likely advantage for observing the drug shipments. I have a planning meeting with them tomorrow. I'll let you know."

"Okay, thanks!" Mary Beth replied. After a few minutes, she asked, "By the way, I don't think we've ever had a Masquerade Ball in this whole area. Do you know why Grace and Joe jumped on the Masquerade Ball idea so quickly for their celebration?"

"Well, that's a good question. It's a wonderful event, but I wonder what made them think of it."

Mary Beth said, "Well, it's crossed my mind that we view it as a very romantic occasion in which you'd meet a complete stranger, dance with them, and end up falling in love. Of course, you had no idea who you danced with because you were each masked, hence, the implausible fairytale ending."

"You're absolutely right," laughed Maggie. "There is no way it would even logically happen. How often have you gone to a party or dance and danced with anyone you didn't know? Never!"

"You're right," Mary Beth agreed. "In my whole life, I've never danced with anyone I didn't know. And what if you came with your date? Or spouse? Or your friend set you up with a blind date? This is hardly an occasion that any sane person would agree to live through."

"However," she continued, "I do really like the dream that you could go to this ball and meet someone who would meet your idealistic qualifications of your soul-mate, sight unseen, and live happily ever after. But in real life, that's impossible."

Maggie agreed wholeheartedly, "Now, if you think about it, I'm sure Grace and Joe don't need to wear masks. They've already found each other and fell in love, although it took them forever to do it. And they didn't have any trouble seeing each other."

"I wonder why a Masquerade Ball has such an imaginary love fantasy pipedream connotation."

Maggie smiled and added, "I have no idea, but I still think it would be fun to go."

"Sure, you get to go with your new husband, James, whom you love dearly."

"I know, but I can't wait. He's the Best!" replied Maggie.

"Oh, please! Spare me! When you met him, you couldn't stand him. You threw him in jail!"

"I know, but that was my first impression, and I didn't even know him. If I met him at a Masquerade Ball, I would never have given him the time of day, much less dance with him!"

"See, that's what I mean."

"Now, here's how my grandmother met my grandfather back in the day."

"Okay, this better be interesting. Did they have a chaperone?"

"Well, you must understand they lived in middle America in the pioneer days. They had a farm where they raised crops. They had some cattle and horses, chickens, a couple of goats, and cows. That's all I heard them talk about. Oh, and a sheepdog.

"In those days, the farmers often helped each other out for the big jobs, like the barn raisings. Building and roofing a complete barn was almost impossible without the extra hired help, so the farmers would take turns helping each other. It was easier and safer to accomplish big jobs like that.

"So, the local farmers got to know each other, although they might not have been close physically. You couldn't walk over to borrow a cup of sugar.

"My grandmother said when she and her sister were teenagers, their family was invited to one of the area farms for a Halloween party. These were more like a Fall Pot-Luck Picnic with games, hay rides, etc. The girls were invited to dress up in costumes if they wanted. That sounded like great fun.

"They spent several days making their costumes in their spare time. The frontier women were very accomplished seamstresses. Sewing and knitting to make their own clothing were necessary abilities in their lives.

"One of my grandmother's talents was artistic. I still have a couple of her paintings in my home. A large one is a framed oil painting of a lake with trees and birds at sunset. It's wonderful. She was self-taught. It must run in the family because her father was a gifted artist with drawings of many animals and people.

"Well, I found a letter of her description of how Grandma painted her face and her sister's face to go to the Halloween party."

"The neighbor's farm was several miles away, so it was an all-day excursion during the daylight hours. They loaded up the horse-drawn carriage and traveled over to their farm.

"A couple of farm families were also invited, and they all had a good time.

"This is how she and her sister had the opportunity to meet and get to know the two teenage boys of the host family. They may have been the only boys they got to hang out with, but they were the two boys my grandma and her sister liked. They ended up getting married.

"They each had good, long marriages with those boys. It helped to have family ties for shared holidays and events. That's how some of the farmers made their lives better."

Chapter Three

Maggie watched her old DEA partner closely. He seemed much quieter than usual. "Hey. I saw you last night dancing with Mary Beth. Then you were gone. What happened? Did she step on your foot or something?"

"Goodness, no!" Antonio responded. "She's a great dancer. Is she a professional?"

"No, but she loves music, and she's taken dance lessons her entire life. She occasionally teaches as a substitute at the Sea Crest Dance Studio. Then, of course, she teaches some special dance classes annually."

"Like what? The tango?" laughed Antonio.

"As a matter of fact, that's one of her favorites. She loves to tango. That's why she started those classes. She needed somebody to tango with!"

"You're kidding, right?"

"No, I'm serious. Now, lots of us know how to tango. One of our favorite music themes was 'The Spanish Tango' from 'The Mask of Zorro.' We all learned it. It was a riot," she laughed before she continued. "If you'd stuck around last night, you'd have seen lots of us dancing. Of course, we're not as good as Mary Beth, but we're good enough to enjoy ourselves."

When Antonio remained in deep thought, she asked, "By the way, what did happen to you last night? You suddenly disappeared."

Maggie prodded when he still didn't answer, "I hope she didn't say anything that upset you. That's hardly like her."

"No, of course, she didn't say anything offensive," he replied crossly. "As a matter of fact, she didn't say anything except, 'Oui,' when I asked her to dance," he said under his breath.

"No kidding! She answered in French? How strange," Maggie exclaimed in alarm.

"Well..., Yes," answered Antonio. "I'd asked her in French, and that's how she answered."

He seemed to marvel out loud as he continued, "It just rolled off her tongue like it was the most natural thing in the world. Then we started to dance, and believe me, I danced with the best of them." He paused, thinking, *"It just never felt so unexpectedly perfect. I'm trying to figure out if it's because I was surprised by how beautiful she looked. However, I have no idea what she looks like without the mask!"*

"Well, I told you she was a good friend of Grace and myself. Of course, her kindness overshadows her attractive good looks."

"I knew she'd had a crush on Zorro, and I guess if I knew that she was, well, someone like Grace. Do you know what I mean? Grace speaks French almost flawlessly. Nothing throws her. She had an answer and the knowledge to back it up for every situation. Well, you know what I mean. I wouldn't have been so eager to play a prank on her. Now, I felt terrible."

"So," said Maggie. "What happened to you?"

"When we danced by the potted trees at the edge of the dance floor, I spun her around into a 1½ turn spin, and

I stepped off the dance floor, behind the potted plants, and kept going. I never looked back!"

Maggie stared at him a full five seconds before she exploded. "Are you kidding me? She's my friend! What on earth were you thinking?"

After a long pause, he explained, "Well, I can't get involved. I didn't know how to get out before I was over my head. So, I just did what I always do. I ended it!"

Maggie was in shock! "Philip, you're an idiot!"

"I am not Philip! I'm Antonio now. That's my new undercover identity. And I can't fall in love with the first person I dance with." That sounded ridiculous even to Antonio.

"Well, I'm sure you just hurt one of my dear friends. No one likes to get dumped in the middle of a beautiful dance. That was downright mean!"

"I'm sorry." He apologized, as he secretly thought, *"Although I'm sure I'll never see her again, so it doesn't really matter. Like catch and release. No harm, No foul. She can't reject me or hurt me. However, I do feel terrible."*

"Well, I sincerely hope you are!"

After a minute, Antonio said, "I've been mapping out some locations that would be perfect for observing the small craft that come ashore. I'm thinking along the lines of me disguised as a beachcomber. I'd build a small beach house near the cliffs where the underground railroad lowered the runaway slaves to the waiting ocean schooners. The ground is pretty rough, and I'd be almost invisible with some camouflaged gear."

"Antonio, having your DEA division join us here at Sea Crest is a privilege. My close friends and family know I've worked with you on several international cases. In fact, the other day, my mom asked me, 'What is a DEA Agent?' I explained that DEA special agents are trained to operate within some of the most dangerous criminal environments imaginable. They may infiltrate criminal organizations as undercover financiers, mediators, or buyers. They may also assume a completely tactical role in some of the federal government's most elite tactical units, the DEA Special Operations Division. In other situations, DEA agents may act as international intelligence operatives collecting information about narcotics organizations from informants, local police organizations, or human intelligence assets."

"Sounds like that just about covers our portfolio of jobs, Maggie," he laughed. "Well done!"

"Yes, I just wanted you to know we are fortunate to have you fighting with us. We can really make an impact together. I wanted to share some of the tools we use at our new location."

Maggie cheerily continued, "The FBI has some of the first to come to market with an anti-reflective device to clip to your binoculars. They have a new Flash Shield to cover the sun glare and won't reflect the sun off your binocular lenses, exposing you to the ones you are spying on. The Flash Shield is the solution to these issues."

"Yes," answered Antonio. "I've got a pair of these and used them in Tahiti. I can put an order in for some additional pairs for this mission."

"Thanks. That would be great!"

The phone rang, and Maggie answered and relayed the message, "Hey, Antonio. Michael Jensen and Joe Lawrence wonder if you could join them at the lighthouse."

"Yeah, sure. Tell them I'll be there in a few minutes."

Chapter Four

Michael greeted Antonio at the Sea Crest Lighthouse door. “Hello, Antonio. Grab a cup of coffee. Joe and I were going up to the top.”

“Thanks! Don’t mind if I do!” replied Antonio as he shook hands with both men and poured his mug.

Joe added, “We do our best thinking at the top of the lighthouse. If you have time, we’d love you to join us.”

“Sounds like a wonderful idea,” replied Antonio with a smile.

Michael held their plans as they headed ‘up top’ with coffee and a rolled-up area map. “We understand you’ve been involved with several Road Rallies in France. Maggie describes your life as exciting by any standard, so we’d like your advice.”

Joe joined in, “As a matter of fact, I looked for you last night at the wedding celebration. You are among the few people we know who have worked on the great French Road Rally version of scavenger hunts. We’d like you to be one of the lead planners of our project. I couldn’t find you last night, but Grace promised you’d have all sorts of creative ideas on how to make it a success.”

Antonio was surprised as he explained, “Sure, I’ll be working out some work details with Maggie, but I’m sure I’ll have some spare time for this. It sounds like a lot of fun. I’m unfamiliar with the various landmarks we should include in our clues. Still, it will help get me acquainted with this beautiful coastal area. Yes! This is right up my alley.”

Joe proudly announced, “My wife, Grace, is the town historian, and she’d love to know the answers to some of the history lost in the hurricane that destroyed so much of our town. We plan to have the scavenger hunt cover the entire Sea Crest community, and we’d like some ideas of historical, interesting, fun, and unusual things for the teams to discover that they never knew existed.

“She has a list of some things you might want to include. We’ll have someone else to help you. Still, according to Maggie, you’re impressive at puzzles and figuring out the various steps for the teams to follow. We hope to expand our tourism to include the Road Rally as an annual event.”

“Sure, I’ll give it a shot. It’s one of my favorite things I do for fun in France.”

Chapter Five

Maggie was setting up her cottage for tomorrow's Mah Jongg game. Her Great Dane, Misha, was following her all around the room. "Misha, I get such a kick out of you. The game's not till tomorrow! It's a riot to watch a large dog like you, still a puppy, run around following me. I love you so much!"

As Maggie set the tiles on the table, Misha recognized that a Mah Jongg game was afoot. Maggie laughed and explained to her excited dog, "Yes, the girls will be over to play our favorite game tomorrow."

The phone started to ring, and as Maggie picked it up, she smiled and said, "Hello, Kate. I'm just setting up for tomorrow's Mah Jongg game."

Kate laughed and said, "Well, tell Misha I'll bring her a treat. However, it will be short and sweet. I can't bring my new puppy, Snarfy, but don't feel bad. We can plan a play date for later in the week.

"Our new neighborhood pug, Louie, is becoming an ideal playmate for Snarfy. His family is flying out of town for a wedding next weekend, and they were kind enough to ask if we'd be interested in having him for an overnight stay. Since they get along so well, I said we'd love the chance to have him over."

"Sounds like fun," replied Maggie. "I'll talk to you later about presenting our anonymous acts of kindness at the Mah Jongg game. I have a couple of ideas to run by you."

Kate said good bye and looked down at Snarfy, who was dancing around her feet. "Do you want to have Louie over for company?" At the mention of the puppy's name, Snarfy jumped around and wagged his tail.

"Alright," laughed Kate, as she informed Snarfy, "calm down. We'll meet them on Friday for a play date, and he'll come home with us. We'll need lots of extra treats and chew toys. And you'll have to share a couple of yours. It will be so much fun!"

Across town, Maggie made a cup of her favorite coffee and dialed Mary Beth's number. "Good morning, Mary Beth. I have a big favor to ask, and I wondered if you could fit it into your busy schedule over the next few weeks."

"Good morning!" replied Mary Beth. "I hope it's to help with the scavenger hunt."

"Well, this is a huge commitment," Maggie explained. "However, I need to ask you to work with a European contact person who both planned and competed in several French Road Rallies."

"Yes! Yes! Yes! I am delighted and excited. I love anything French! I was hoping you'd ask me!"

"We couldn't even think of anyone else that could do the job you could. Thank you so much!

"When do I meet the other party I'll be working with?"

"I think Michael Jensen was planning to track them down this morning. I'll let you know when I hear back."

"Great. I've got a couple of things to do this morning, too. I'll have my phone with me. See you later, and I'm thrilled."

"Bye, see you later."

Chapter Six

Later that afternoon, Antonio walked up to the Sea Crest Church. While wandering around the grounds, he found the old section of the cemetery, which included monuments and markers over a century old. The graves were from back to the original Sir Michael Chambers and many important sailors from the past.

He wandered into an area of centuries-old grave markers. Many date back to The Golden Days of Pirates on the high seas. Although he wasn't up to speed on the names, he was able to make out interesting epitaphs by some notable pirates. William Kidd, or "Captain Kidd" as he is often remembered, was one of the most renowned privateers and pirates of this era, along with Blackbeard and Black Bart.

The fact that these graves couldn't possibly be the actual resting place of all these pirates and smugglers was not lost on Antonio. These famous pirates had their names on graves scattered in numerous towns up and down the coastal waters. Antonio had been an undercover DEA agent for long enough to recognize that these burial plots also probably did not contain the remains of all of these pirates either. However, it made them look like they'd famously been part of Sea Crest's history.

Antonio stopped at a tombstone with a compass pointing due north etched above the inscription. He knelt and read softly to himself,

'Gold is a constant,
like the North Star.'

The next marker read:

X always marks the spot,
even if it's underwater
RIP
Blackbeard

A few steps away, under a giant oak tree, Antonio encountered a gravestone that showed an etching of an ugly pirate wielding a sword. He had wild black hair and fierce eyes. His swirling mustache was long, and the curling ends were on fire! Antonio jumped back, *"Good Grief! That's one of the most bizarre graves I've ever seen! Not that I've frequented very many cemeteries."*

Edward "Blackbeard" Teach
Rest in Peace
'Blackbeard was feared,
His appearance was weird.'
'Lost his gold ship,
where the sea floor dipped.'

"Wow, does that mean that Blackbeard buried his treasure here? Grace never mentioned anything about pirates!"

"I doubt he's buried here, but these pirates stowed their bounty in many areas. Most of Blackbeard's treasures were never recovered, although the hunt has continued for centuries. This is something that

Maggie has never discussed with me. Will this issue be part of my DEA project?"

As Antonio exited that pirate section of the cemetery, he approached a newer area from the Civil War era. The headstones seemed to date from the construction of the Sea Crest Lighthouse and the early founders of the surrounding area.

He was putting this information together as he walked. *"These must include the ancestors of the seaside community of Sea Crest. These would probably include Maggie and Grace's families."*

"Wow, this tombstone reads that the man died looking for the gold from the missing railroad cars from the Civil War." Antonio realized, "Boy, I better do some research because I'm unfamiliar with some of America's Civil War details. When I was in school, I moved around a lot in Europe. However, while I was stranded with Grace on that uninhabited island in Tahiti, she never shared any information about a train carrying a gold shipment, which was lost and missing."

As Antonio walked closer to the cliff's edge, he looked down at the waves crashing at the water's edge and was astonished at the site. *"Wow, that's the old railroad tracks the way they were shown and pictured on the original land maps at Maggie's headquarters. These are century-old abandoned railroad tracks recently exposed by storm damage. Ironically, they are located on the sandy beach about fifty feet below where the Underground R.R. ended. No one has discovered this newly uncovered shoreline because it is hidden in the cliffs, past the Sea Crest Lighthouse."*

He continued to view the land where the railroad tracks were now in plain sight. He toyed with the idea of renovating the old rail car half-buried in the sandy debris. *"The 'Tiny House' phenomenon is of great interest to me. My creative side is fascinated with how people can make and repurpose the most outlandish shelters out of complete wrecks. It's getting dark out, and I'll soon have to leave so I can find my way back."*

He marked the trail to ensure he doesn't get lost trying to find the railroad tracks when he returns tomorrow to investigate further.

He wishes the town of Sea Crest hadn't lost all the historical records. *"I think I'll check online tonight and see if there are any archives from the nearby towns that might show stories of the missing Gold Train or the prospector who was looking for the Gold and was now buried at the Sea Crest Church Cemetery.*

"I remember watching a documentary about the old abandoned train tunnels worldwide. The guide showed many astounding creations of structures that have been hidden from sight for decades.

"The guide usually wore no gloves for his investigations, no matter how cold it was. However, his advice was to always wear boots of some kind. Since I wear sandals mostly around water, I figured if I was ever lucky enough to inspect a tunnel, I'd listen to the expert on this one."

This memory brought a smile to his face. *"I admire the adventurous approach of this guide. His talk was fascinating and presented so well that it sparked a seed of encouragement to try it yourself, however, with the safety that his knowledge and example provided.*

"The contents of these videos were very well photographed, with abundant lighting that made it simple to see what he was describing, even in the least accessible corners of the edifices he was targeting. These areas were engaging and focused on areas that we never have a view of. I was thoroughly entertained the whole time.

"One of the surprises I was most educated on was the forgotten network of tunnels. The connection of knowledge of civil engineering and how it works with the natural world was remarkable, to say the least.

"The rock tunnels are some of my favorites. Especially when they are carved out of the rock in a design that shows the colors and textures. I also love the fascinating rock formations, and the kinds of

stones are incredible. Many are found in the local region where they are used. I have a new appreciation of ordinary things right before me, but I never really thought about them before.

"Since viewing those wonderful episodes, I've sought out a few abandoned train tunnel adventures myself. They are astonishing; I wish I'd had someone to share my enthusiasm with.

"I remember one discovery of a tunnel that led to an adjoining tunnel that was so primitive that it had no structural support. I didn't go far into it because the ceiling showed no bricking or metal, and I found it extremely unsafe. It also had quite a bit of water to wade through. However, the strange tunnel had survived for a very long time. I was just scared to advance further in that dangerous situation. Now, if I had someone with me, maybe I could talk them into going further. I'd be standing guard to go for help if the whole thing collapsed on them.

"I'm glad I could find some of these older tunnels. I imagine the train designs were too large for the older tunnels, so I understand why they had to upgrade, especially with older ones already deteriorating with time. It's a shame they couldn't keep up with the repairs if they were growing obsolete. This old rock tunnel looked awesome, and how great was it that the rail ties were still there. I hope to find other evidence of these ties that are still around and somehow being preserved by the cold and the water.

"This is going to be wonderful to discover the local history of these the old railroad lines. I also hope to see if there is evidence of graffiti and what it can tell us about its history.

"I will find out if this hasn't been a part of the Rails to Trails program. As for the tunnel system, it might. I bet it'd be too risky to allow many people near for safety reasons."

The sun was setting as Antonio shook his head and slowly turned to leave. He marveled at his surprising find as he departed. He looked around and noticed this beach area was secluded and hidden from the shoreline. As he climbed to higher ground, he saw the beautiful waves crashing along the beach. It was positively breathtaking. *"What an amazing day!"*

However, what he didn't notice, hidden from view, was a small fishing boat. Two men were concealed by lying flat on the bottom of his boat. The third man, steering the craft, carefully watched Antonio's every move out of the corner of his eyes. They made sure they did not steer toward the area where he was located. The man steering observed, "Boy, I hope this guy isn't a problem. I'd hate to deal with unwanted obstacles on this job."

"Yes," agreed Jack, who was tucked down, safe from view, under a tarp. "It's almost dark. Let's return early tomorrow and see if he returns before we set up this as our permanent spot."

"Okay," responded Charlie, the other hidden fellow. "We should arrive early and be prepared to deal with him if he returns."

"Hey, you guys! I don't want any trouble. This coastline goes on for miles! We don't have to work out of this area."

"Wrong!" said Charlie. "This is the only exposed area of the rails and abandoned rail cars."

"Yeah." Jack explained, "Don't forget about the lost gold shipment."

"Well, don't forget we're using my boat," Bill pointed out. "We don't want any trouble."

Chapter Seven

Later that evening, Antonio settled down at his computer to research the Lost Gold. He chuckled as he thought, *"Every tale that has stood the test of time has some nugget of truth, so let's see what this missing gold shipment is all about."*

He first explored what he could discover from related searches about the event. He muttered as he scrolled through the information. "According to this history site, this happened in April 1865 when the Union troops closed in on Richmond, Virginia. President Jefferson Davis and the Confederates fled South, taking with them a huge shipment of gold, silver, and other coins. But alas, when the Northern officers caught up with Davis on May 10, he had no riches.

"What actually happened to that missing Confederate treasure has remained a mystery. Instead of answers, we are left with every conceivable theory that could be imagined for over 150 years."

Antonio wondered, *"Fine, but what about the railroad tracks?"*

"Let's see; this article by their Attorney Cluck explains that a new Pennsylvania court ruling could help private treasure hunters in their quest to learn if the FBI dug up a fabled cache of lost Civil War gold. There seems to be some mystery about whether the FBI dug up about $400 million from a remote Pennsylvania forest nearly three years ago. In 2018, they excavated an area in Dent's Run of Elk County that was sealed from public view.

"This resulted from a U.S. judge unsealing the case records and using the Right-To-know Law appeal to obtain information. It seems that Attorney Cluck was representing a treasure-hunting company that directed the Feds to the site, where they dug a hole and hit something promising. His clients felt entitled to share in the gold possibly found and removed by the government.

"The clandestine maneuver was generated from the Battle of Gettysburg in July 1863 when the Union Army shipped a consignment of gold to Philadelphia consisting of 26 or 52 gold bars, each weighing 50 pounds. This heavy load was between 1,300 and 2,600 pounds.

"The veil of secrecy and suspicious behavior has created an ongoing mysterious legend because the gold never arrived at its destination. The missing shipment was lost, stolen, buried, or hidden away, attracting and captivating treasure hunters for over 150 years.

"The claimants that the ground-penetrating survey showed something big was buried in the Dent's Run location. Eyewitnesses saw over 50 agents that were there all night with armored cars. They are convinced they have found the gold!"

Antonio was intrigued, to say the least, as he thought out his next move. *"Well, it's getting late, but I'm excited to retrace my steps to recheck the railroad tracks in the morning."*

Chapter Eight

As it turns out, three very concerned guys were trying to figure out how to scare this tourist away from their latest project.

"What if he shows up tomorrow?"

"If this slips through our hands, that's the end for us. Do you guys have any ideas," asked Jack?

"I'm not sure what we should do," answered Bill. "However, we should verify whose gold we are searching for. The railroad tracks reminded us of the old story of the 'Lost Gold' sent to Philadelphia in 1863 but never arrived. Each Gold Brick weighed 50 pounds. That's so heavy that if it ever weighed down the rail cars, it would be easy to derail the train."

Charlie pointed out, "Don't forget about Blackbeard's Treasure. They still haven't found most of his reported treasure. That's my guess. I think it's related to Blackbeard's missing gold."

"What makes you say that," asked Jack?

Charlie answered, "Very little has been written about the early life of privateer-turned-pirate Edward 'Blackbeard' Teach. He was an active pirate for a brief spell in the early 18th century. He became famous for being ugly with his massive, knotted beard and horrible appearance. He burned the ends of his mustache with fire to singe and curl them. His black hair stuck out every which way. He didn't wash or bathe for weeks, so he would stink and smell obnoxious. He had a reputation as the most ruthless pirate alive, and he struck fear in seamen's hearts throughout the Caribbean and Eastern United States. However, his legend has grown even stronger with time, keeping the hunt for his supposed hidden treasure alive."

Bill jumped in with his observation, "Most historians suspect that Teach (like most pirates) didn't get around to making desert-island deposits of gold and jewels during his reign, but there are still several places where, given what we've learned about him in the past three centuries, the treasure could have ended up."

Charlie added, "I recall that it might have ended up off the coast of North Carolina. That's where his ship, Queen Anne's Revenge, was damaged beyond repair. Some historians think Blackbeard had up to 10 days to offload supplies before it finally sank.

"Of course, it could also be scattered anywhere in the Caribbean. He only operated briefly as a pirate on the high seas in 1717 and 1718. Blackbeard was busy at sea, reportedly ransacking or capturing approximately 30 ships."

Bill asked, "Do either of you know about the Plum Point possible location of some of his treasure?"

"That sounds familiar, but I'm not sure of the reason why."

Bill explained, "I heard it was because when Blackbeard was trying to make it as a regular, non-pirate person after his pardon, he set up shop near Governor Eden's homestead in Bath, North Carolina. His bayside home on Plum Point has since drawn treasure hunters and shovels to the town. I doubt he buried his treasure here, but I'll bet some is stashed there.

Charlie added, "I've read that Blackbeard freed many slaves during his piracy career, but he wasn't an abolitionist. Many ships he captured were slave ships, which tended to be larger to account for maximum 'cargo.' Upon capture, Blackbeard apparently gave them a choice to work with his crew, and many slaves joined the pirates. I'm unsure if their alternative was killing them, forcing them overboard, or selling them as a slave at the next port. Either way, the ship's treasure was not always gold and silver."

"Governor Eden, who pardoned Blackbeard after deliberately grounding his ship, gave the pirate one of his confiscated ships back and even helped Teach get established in Bath Creek. It's long been speculated that the Governor was on the take regarding Teach's profitable piracy. Legend has it that Blackbeard was able to slip easily in and out of Eden's estate (presumably to deliver the governor's cut of the loot) by using a particular rock path or, in some versions, an underground passage between Bath Creek and Eden's, Archbell Point home."

"As a last resort, maybe, Blackbeard's gold is still being safely kept down below. Somewhere a lot deeper than even the very bottom shelf of Davy Jones' Locker," stated Charlie.

Chapter Nine

Mary Beth was on cloud nine as she opened the door to her costume room, which housed an assortment of beautiful natural hair wigs and adornments. She placed the deluxe quality women's short black wig from the Masquerade Ball on its pedestal rack. She fluffed the side-swept fringe of the bob, which swung longer in the front to frame the face as she said, "There, now that looks great."

"Nonetheless, I must stop concentrating on last night and think about my new responsibility of planning for the scavenger hunt," she decided firmly. She thought about the clues they'd find at the Sea Crest Cemetery. Graves from the town's original founders, plus the Sea Crest Lighthouse, were in the Sea Crest Church's Cemetery. *"We'll find many other symbols dating back to the mid-1800s on grave markers, such as An Anchor, which means Hope for a sailor or captain. Also, an anchor with a broken chain means this life ended too soon."*

Mary Beth was turning over the various options in her mind. *"I'm looking forward to choosing clues from the graves of those buried during the Golden Age of Piracy. We have the burial place for Black Beard and several other famous sailors."*

Her melancholy feelings returned to the incredible dance with Zorro at the Masquerade Ball. *"I still can't forget the light, wonderful feeling I felt as we danced. I wonder where he came from, who he is, and if I'll ever see him again. I also wonder why he disappeared."*

Mary Beth decided to stop thinking about him. "Well, enough of that; I must prepare for the day ahead!"

She continued into the walk-in closet where her dresses were hanging and selected one of her sun dresses. She picked one that was nice to wear for the planned day. As she dressed, she viewed her image in the full-length mirror. *"This sundress's tiny green pattern is fresh and lovely."*

She twirled around as she remembered the thrill of her very first childhood dance lessons. *"I always love to dress up for the recitals and watch the costumes flow to the music. This is just the look I want!*

"Today, I have to meet my partner in planning the Scavenger Hunt, and I want to look fun and competent. I think this will do nicely. I love the short, flared bell-shaped sleeves with a ruffle. It closes seamlessly as the dress wraps around to form a V-neck in the front, plus ties at the waist complete the bottom part of the bodice."

She confidently complimented herself aloud, "If I do say so myself, it's a perfect fit and very flattering."

She ran her fingers down the delicate edging as she admired the reflection in the mirror. *"Yes, the finishing touch is this playful wide ruffle along the edge that cascades loosely down, falls gracefully just off center, and continues along the bottom of the hem. This design is chic and elegant."*

Her thoughts continued as she hummed happily. *"This casual summer dress is perfect for viewing a new real estate listing I have this morning before the meeting. In fact, I think I'll stop by Maggie's office and see if they have any new information about the Sea Crest Scavenger Hunt.*

"I'm looking forward to meeting the person they selected to share the planning of the scavenger hunt with me. They've been to several French Road rallies. I hope they agree to work with me on the Scavenger hunt."

She smiled as she looked in the mirror. She wore sunscreen and minimal makeup except for her big baby blue eyes. She quickly added an additional application of mascara to make them pop.

She combed her blond sun-bleached waves and felt, *"I'm sure glad I had my hair cut and shaped to pull off the wind-swept look I need in my coastal life here at Sea Crest. No matter what the weather throws at me, my hair wisps, locks, and wavy tresses will fall into place no matter if I'm in braids, ponytails, pigtails, or a one-sided ponytail; it waves and blows with the sea breezes."*

Chapter Ten

Antonio was up early and drove to a nearby town to research their courthouse records for any information regarding abandoned railroad tracks or railroad cars in the Sea Crest area. By ten o'clock, he had the necessary information he was looking for. It has been decades since a railroad ran through the Sea Crest coastal community, and it appeared that no one was any the wiser.

No one would have any way of looking for the missing gold train because it wasn't known to have traveled in this corridor. What an exciting turn of events.

He made copies of details of several of the Golden Age of Pirates to compare with the info on the grave markers.

Antonio reviewed some of the information in his mind as he drove. *"It didn't seem realistic, and the timelines didn't align correctly to have them die and be buried at Sea Crest. However, this was an ideal place to hide their bounty. The available records agreed that you couldn't put your valuables in a bank in those days. It was also not plausible to believe pirates could keep the super-heavy gold bars on board their ships. They needed vessels that could be swift and navigate through all kinds of fast maneuverings.*

"The possibility of having an enemy ship steal all the treasure on board was another problem.

"Digging a hole and burying it or keeping it all in the exact location was also not smart. Much of the coastline was rocky, and digging a large hole where you could find it again would have been hard."

He was pleased as he drove into the Sea Crest Church parking lot and parked Maggie's car. "What a beautiful day!"

He located the vantage point from yesterday and started down the rocky hillside, picking his way down the banks to the sandy shoreline.

It took him a while to arrive at the exposed railroad tracks. *"Oh, there is the old rail car."*

As he approached that area, he thought, *"Wow. More than one rail car is peeking out from sand dunes and debris. I'll bet this train derailed at the time of impact. It looks like a massive pile of giant pick-up sticks."*

He continued investigating and finally entered the tipped-over rail car to look around. He heard a sound and turned just in time to get slammed in the head with a piece of driftwood.

Chapter Eleven

Meanwhile, Mary Beth had arrived at Maggie's office but found her missing. She promptly approached Maggie's desk to see what she was working on. Her amazed eyes scanned the newspaper clippings, including the railroad information. "Wow!" she mumbled. "The old Sea Crest Railroad now has exposed tracks. I can't believe it. I never even heard of a railroad around here."

It suddenly occurred to her that this person was trying to investigate the details of the Rally without her. *"Well, I'm going to see what they are up to,"* she decided as she headed out the door.

Mary Beth leisurely walked down the pebbled beach toward the cliffs, armed with her clipboard and pen. She carefully took notes on landmarks that would fit into the French Rally-themed scavenger hunt she was organizing. She stopped to shield her eyes and gazed at the Sea Crest Lighthouse. The sea breeze swept her blond-streaked hair over her pretty, tanned face.

Her sundress was perfect for this stroll along the sand as the tide played its rhythmic dance along the shore. She suddenly chuckled as she remembered what had happened the last time she had worn this outfit.

"One of the tourists came running up to me with delight, "Excuse me, may I have your autograph? My sister and I have seen all your movies. Of course, her sister insisted that 'Over Board,' as a real-life couple, her husband Kurt Russell was the funniest. However, they also liked 'House sitter' with Steve Martin. Who doesn't love Chevy Chase with her in 'Foul Play' and 'Seems like old times.'

"Oh well, all kidding aside. It was fun having them mistake me for Goldie Hawn. They laughed excitedly when I signed their note paper; 'with all my love, Annie, Gwen, Gloria Mundy, and Glenda Parks.'

"What a gift to get to live in this beautiful town.

"The tourist season is going to be spectacular this summer. We are having this Scavenger Hunt to support the new Sea Crest Lighthouse Museum, which will explain and honor the rich maritime history of our town."

She loved working in the small seaside town's museum, and this event was shaping up to be a great fundraiser. Mary Beth traveled along the cliff area until she came to the newly exposed tracks and railroad cars. The sand dunes and debris were challenging to navigate. As she slowly made her way closer, she discovered an old rail car partially buried in a sand dune. She was so thrilled as she thought, *"Cool! This resembles an old beach shack, dilapidated by years of saltwater battering."*

As she got closer, she spotted a large, crumbling, damaged opening in the side. She carefully moved the sagging board out of her way, and as she crept in, she saw something that made her heart drop to her stomach. Mary Beth approached a man lying on the floor, moaning softly. "Well, thank God, he's alive," she realized. She inched closer, with utmost caution, wondering who he was and what had happened to him.

A man lay face down on the sandy, dirty floor with a blood-stained wound on his forehead.

She inched closer, wondering who he was and what had happened to him. Her CPR and first aid training kicked in as she felt for a pulse and checked his breathing. *"Okay, it's shallow, but it's there."*

Quickly, she dialed 911 and tried to keep the man conscious. However, he was too groggy and disoriented.

Chapter Twelve

His voice was barely audible as he moaned, "Help me!" He tried to shift his body toward the approaching movement. He held his forehead as the sharp pain sliced through his head again. "What is happening?"

Mary Beth whispered, "Try to lie perfectly still. Help is on the way."

Antonio was waking up to find his world in utter chaos.

Mary Beth was waiting for the operator to answer while she looked for a tissue in her fanny pack. "I will apply pressure to stop the bleeding on your forehead. Okay?"

"Yes, I guess."

The 911 operator picked up and asked for her location.

"Hello, I'm at the shoreline, below the cliffs, out beyond the Sea Crest Lighthouse. We have a man down. He's got a gash on his forehead, which is bleeding. I'm bandaging his head to put pressure on the cut on his forehead."

She tore the ruffle from her sundress that ran down the front fold of her dress. The seam remained holding the dress closed, but the ruffle separated, and she could remove about a yard of decorative ribbon-like material. Mary Beth folded a bandage-like cushion over the wound and wrapped the long ruffle around his head to apply pressure.

Mary Beth continued, "He's lying on the floor of what looks like an old railroad car. I don't think he can be moved without medical help."

She waited a minute for further instructions. "Okay, I'll check," she replied.

She turned to the man on the floor, "The Coast Guard Search and Rescue Team is on the way. They need to know what your name is and what happened here."

He turned his head and looked perplexed, thinking, *"What's my name? Nothing comes to mind. I wonder what it is!"* He was drawing a complete blank as he finally uttered in shock, "I have no idea!"

They just stared at each other momentarily when he continued, "And here's another small detail we should clear up if you don't mind!" He tried to sit up but fell helplessly back on the floor. "What's your name, and did you just clobber me with something?"

Chapter Thirteen

Mary Beth was stunned as she practically yelled into her phone, "Now he demands 'What's my name'? 'Did I just clobber him with something?'" She tried to calm down as she stared him straight in the eyes and angrily asked, "Are you kidding me? I'm trying to help you!"

She immediately felt sorry for practically yelling at him. "I'm sorry. I didn't hit you with anything. I was searching for these half-buried, abandoned railroad tracks. I discovered that they have recently been exposed by the recent storm in this area."

He responded weakly, "Well, I can't remember anything about myself or why I'm here. Oh, now I hear the sirens. I guess you really did call 911 for help."

The helicopter pilot crawled into the small space as the Coast Guard Search and Rescue team descended beside the rail car on the coast. Captain Kate Jensen knelt beside her friend, Mary Beth, and observed that she was holding the hand of the injured man on the floor.

"Well, the plot thickens." Kate looked into the face of the new undercover DEA agent. It took her a split second to decide what to do. She calmly addressed everyone, "I know this is

unusual, but I'm going to ask if you could all step back outside for a few minutes. I need to ask this man a few questions. Don't worry: I'll let you all back in to help in a minute."

Mary Beth was reluctant to leave him for some ridiculous reason. She whispered, "Kate, I think he might have amnesia. I don't know what happened to him, but he doesn't know who he is or why he's here. Can I stay?"

Kate looked down at their hands and softly explained, "I'll need a few minutes with him. He'll be okay."

Mary Beth let go of his hand, which she didn't even know she had been holding. As she left to go outside with the others, she thought, *"Boy, is this ever strange."*

Kate took Mary Beth's place and knelt to tell him, "Hello. I'm a Coast Guard helicopter pilot. I'll let the Search and Rescue team back in soon, and they'll help get you out of here. I just wanted to ask you if you know who you are?"

Sadly, he replied, "I don't know my name, why I'm here, or why someone or something hit me in the head. That lady said she didn't hit me. Do you believe her?"

"Yes, you can absolutely trust and believe her. We grew up together, and she's one of my best friends."

Chapter Fourteen

Kate stepped outside the half-exposed shack and directed the team to get him ready to transport. In the meantime, she boarded the helicopter and made a private call to Maggie.

"Hello, Maggie,"

"Hi, what's up?"

"Well, I've got some bad news for you."

"Oh no, what happened?"

"I'm on the Sea Crest shoreline beneath the cliffs. Mary Beth called in a 911 call for a man who was lying face down on the ground inside a railroad car on the newly exposed railroad tracks. He's conscious now, but he's got amnesia. He asked me if Mary Beth was the one who hit him over the head with something."

"Oh no! We have an undercover DEA agent up there today. He was investigating the area for a possible lookout location for drug smugglers," replied Maggie.

"Well, this guy is a dead ringer for Philip, who was working undercover in Tahiti."

"Yeah, that's our guy!"

"Well," Kate said. "I'm going to let the rest of the rescue team get him out of here, but we won't blow his cover. We are going to call him John Doe until his memory returns. We can fly him to a secure location at our Coast Guard Medical Center and patch his forehead. We can also provide him with some expert help to regain his memory."

Kate looked around as she invited the team back in. She asked the team, "Did any of you move that heavy piece of driftwood beside him?"

"No!"

"Good."

Then she asked Antonio, "Will you be okay for a couple more minutes? I want to take some pictures of crime scenes before we move you. Can you handle a minute or two more if it helps us solve who did this to you?"

"Yes. I think that would be okay."

"Great. We'll be quick, but we must take advantage of all the facts we can gather."

She turned to the crew member nearest her and instructed, "Next, bag up that driftwood so we can dust it for prints."

The Search and Rescue personnel quickly secured Antonio for his helicopter trip.

Kate asked Mary Beth, "Can you please join us for the helicopter flight to the Coast Guard Medical Center?"

"Oh, I just walked over from Maggie's FBI headquarters."

Kate quickly explained, "I don't think it's safe here. Maggie is sending some FBI agents and Sea Crest Police Officers to see if they can catch whoever assaulted this man."

Mary Beth took her place inside. As she heard the swish of the helicopter blades as the helicopter lifted, she focused on the man on the stretcher. She thought, *"Something extraordinary is going on. Why aren't they taking him to The Sea Crest Medical Center?"*

Chapter Fifteen

The SARS helicopter set down on the Coast Guard Medical Center helipad.

Kate explained to the center's medical team, "This man is to be registered as 'John Doe' to protect his identity. The only ones who will be allowed to know his true I.D. will be me, FBI Special Agent Maggie Jensen, and the doctor who will treat him. He has amnesia and probably a concussion, as well."

"It looks like his vitals have improved," stated a nurse as they wheeled him into the private room in the ER.

"That's nice. I'll stay here until the Emergency Room doctor gives a detailed examination and see if his amnesia is the extent of his injuries. Protocol," continued Kate, "will be structured around his safety and set up immediately by the FBI."

The doctor introduced himself as he entered the private examination room with a chart. "Hello, my name is Doctor Lewis. I understand you were found by the railroad tracks along the Sea Crest coastline. Let me take a look at that gash on your forehead.

"Good, let me put a couple of stitches in that wound; it should heal nicely."

As the doctor worked on the forehead, he casually asked, "I've found that this type of injury usually has some possible side effects. One is a temporary memory loss, and the other is a concussion. I think you have both."

"Well, I know I got whacked in the head, and I don't remember much."

The doctor finished the surgery and asked, "Do you remember the name, 'Philip'?"

"I don't think so. It doesn't sound bad, but I don't recognize it as my name.

"Well, you recently changed your undercover name to Antonio. Does that sound familiar?

"I like that name a lot," he actually smiled. "It reminds me of Zorro. However, again, it doesn't sound exactly right."

"What about the name Maggie? Does that mean anything to you?"

"No, but I like it. Is she my girlfriend or my wife?" he asked as he looked at his ring finger for evidence of marriage.

Kate laughed, "You two have been excellent partners on several international cases. She just got married a short time ago to a wonderful man."

The doctor was pleasantly surprised; *Antonio's hopeful disposition would be very beneficial as he tried to figure everything out.*

Kate continued, "No one needs to know any information I just shared with you. I'll tell Maggie because you're working with her at Sea Crest. Until you recover your memory, you'll be going under the name of John Doe."

Before the doctor left, Antonio had one more strange thing to share. "There is one thing that seemed familiar, but it wasn't a name. It's about that lady. You know the one. What is the name of that lady that found me?"

"Well," Kate spoke up. "We're not at liberty to disclose that for her safety. Whoever hit you with that driftwood knows she found you. Until we know she won't be harmed, we don't think it will be okay for you to know too much about her."

The doctor was alarmed by that remark and said, "If that person seems familiar, that may be just what would help you regain your memory. Tell me about what you heard or felt when she found you."

"I detected a faint smell of Chanel N°5," he whispered in amazement. "I know it sounds ridiculous, but it made me feel great! I don't even know why I know that scent, but it made me want to be near her," he marveled. "However, when I opened my eyes and looked at her, I didn't know her. I didn't realize that I had a memory loss, but I immediately thought she was the one that had clobbered me with something heavy."

Kate asked the following question that surprised him. "Do you remember when I arrived in the helicopter?"

"Yes, I think I was glad that she really had called for help even though I thought she had hit me," he admitted sheepishly.

"When I walked in, you were holding her hand, and I don't think either of you was even aware of it."

Chapter Sixteen

A short time later, Maggie arrived at the Coast Guard Medical Center to see how she could help her dear friend, Antonio. She explained to Doctor Lewis, the amnesia specialist, "Antonio has amnesia, and he doesn't know who he is! That is a big problem on many levels. I've known him for years and worked hand in hand with him on international drug problems around the world. He is at the highest level of the International Drug Enforcement Agency. As the Federal Bureau of Investigation Special Agent from the USA, I was assigned to join the task force to solve several global problems. This is a very dangerous situation!"

"Of course," replied the doctor. "I'll set him on a path to recovery, but it may take time."

"Look, I've known Antonio for years, and he's the best. However, I think he's at risk of being killed without remembering how to survive and care for himself. I believe he wouldn't have been left alive if Mary Beth hadn't interrupted the attack at the beach. Now, one of my best friends is also in danger. In fact, the assailants probably think she actually saw them and can identify them."

Doctor Lewis pondered this sobering information in silence for a moment. After considering the seriousness of this situation, he spoke with deep concern, "What I'm going to suggest is what I think might be the fastest remedy for Antonio's memory, but it's also the most dangerous."

"What do you have in mind?" asked Maggie fearfully.

The doctor said softly, "You're not going to like it, but I'll share what I believe will be the most effective path to take."

Maggie whispered, "I appreciate your honesty. Please, time is of the essence."

The doctor said, "Okay. I believe that may be key since Antonio has some unknown connection to this woman, Mary Beth, who found him. It's not in his consciousness but in his heart somehow."

He paused as though confused but continued, "It's purely a feeling at this point. However, it's in some conflict. He felt it before he actually saw her with his eyes. No, it doesn't match his feelings. He either knows something represents a wrong or guilt. His mind says No! But his heart was still not agreeing as he took her hand, even when his mind held the belief that she was the one that hit him. He held her hand."

Maggie had not heard about this quirky admission that anyone had felt familiar to Antonio. "Where are you getting this data from?"

"Let me look at my notes. Let's see, here it is; 'When I was finishing stitching up his forehead, Antonio said he didn't have any memories, but, and I quote, 'Only one thing seemed the least bit familiar, and it wasn't a name. ... What is the name of that lady that found me?"

"Then Kate said, 'We're not at liberty to disclose that for her safety. Whoever hit you with that driftwood knows she found you. Until we verify that she's not going to be harmed, we don't think it will be okay for you to know too much about her.'

"I was alarmed by that remark, so I stepped in and encouraged him to share. If that person seems familiar, that may be just what would help you regain your memory. Tell me about what you heard or felt when she found you."

"This is word-for-word: Antonio whispered in amazement, 'I detected a faint smell of Chanel No. 5. I know it sounds ridiculous, but it made me feel great! I don't even know why I know that scent, but it made me want to be near her,' he marveled. 'However, when I opened my eyes and looked at her, I didn't know her. I didn't realize that I had a memory loss, but I immediately thought she was the one that had clobbered me with something heavy.'"

"Wow! I think I know why he feels this way!" Maggie exclaimed as she clapped her hands in delight.

"Okay, now it's your turn. What have you got?"

Maggie told all she knew about their reaction to each other at the Masquerade Ball at the Sea Crest Lighthouse. How Antonio was so attracted to her that he left Mary Beth in the middle of the dance floor and escaped by way of the potted plants. "Of course, he doesn't recognize her. She wore a short black bob wig that framed her face on the sides and a higher bob in the back. She wore a silver flapper costume and always wore various Chanel perfumes, lotion, or hair spray. But it's sparse and barely noticeable unless you're close."

"Close, like in dancing or bandaging your head with the ruffle of your dress?" smiled Doctor Lewis. "Now you've just opened a crack in the window of Antonio's physic."

"And for the record, Mary Beth naturally resembles Goldie Hawn. She's been mistaken for her several times during tourist season. She looks nothing like the flapper Antonio danced with at the Masquerade Ball."

"Does Mary Beth know Antonio?" asked Doctor Lewis.

"No. She wasn't expecting a masked man, disguised as Zorro, to ask her to dance. She wondered where he'd gone since he disappeared before the dance ended. She didn't see him again for the entire evening."

"Do you think she recognized him?"

"No, she would have told Kate or me."

"Well," Doctor Lewis said. "The most productive step we should take is to get them together in a safe environment and see if we can develop some memories. They could go for a walk in a familiar area."

"We could tell Mary Beth that Antonio was supposed to meet with her today. He was the person who had agreed to co-plan and organize the Scavenger Hunt with a French Road-Rally format. It's a fundraiser for the Sea Crest Museum. Neither one of them knew who the other person who they'd be working with was, but they were each excited to work on the event."

"That's a splendid idea. We'll tell them they must review some ideas and walk the area together. Of course, we'll have people in place to ensure they are each safe."

"Great! We can pitch the idea as a productive effort to possibly help Antonio's memory by reminding and placing him in some of his favorite pastimes in France. That should go a long way in breaking the ice between them and exploring their shared love of France and all things French. They have so much in common."

"Yes, we could monitor things in the area to ensure their safety while they can get to know each other."

"Perfect!" said Dr Lewis. "It may be prudent to have them do a walk-through of a small village near the Coast Guard Medical Center as a trial run. One of the bakeries/coffee shops has a delightful custom of serving afternoon tea at 4 o'clock.

It's reminiscent of 'High Tea,' allowing them to sit and relax over tea or coffee. It's a tradition that's not lost in Europe. It might bring on some memories to sit and 'talk for a spell.'"

"Sounds like a good idea."

"Maggie, will you have time to assemble a security detail this afternoon?"

"Yes! I can have Mary Beth meet him at The Tea Café around 3:30. I'm sure she'll have her clipboard ready to plan the scavenger hunt."

Chapter Seventeen

The sweet aroma filled the air and awakened her senses as Mary Beth entered The Tea Café. *"What a feeling!"*

She breathed in the sheer joy of it all. *"I hope I never forget the pleasure I get from French cakes and baked delicacies. This unexpected suggestion that I meet the other scavenger hunt planner here was a gift. 'Best Day Ever!'*

"That makes up for the part about it being Antonio. I sure didn't see that coming. Oh, there he is. He's spotted me, so I'd better join him."

Mary Beth waved as she approached his table for two.

He immediately stood up, "Hello! I'm so glad you could come." He smiled as he pulled out a seat for her.

"Thanks, I love this shop," she smiled as she sat down. "I've never been to this little village before. I love the tree-lined streets. It resembles a picture book with the flowers in baskets on the lampposts. It's delightful."

They cautiously tried to make conversation, although they were absolute strangers.

"I know what you mean. All the charm is unexpected to me, even though it might be normal. I don't remember much about my past, but this town feels good. By the way, Thanks for saving my life today."

"Oh, anyone would have done the same! Are you feeling okay?"

Antonio touched the bandaged stitches on his tender forehead. "I am now. Thank you for bandaging my head to stop the bleeding. The doctor said you did something vital. He said it looked like some fancy long ruffled material, but it worked great."

"Yes, it was off my dress. I just ripped the ruffle off and used it. I often do impulsive things if I get impatient or.... scared." Mary Beth whispered.

"Well, meeting you under more pleasant circumstances is a pleasure."

"I agree. We were scheduled to meet today to work on the French Rally-style Scavenger Hunt. It's a fundraiser for The Sea Crest Museum."

"Yes. That's what they told me. It's one reason they wanted us to get acquainted this afternoon. They said I know something about France and if we meet at this shop with High Tea at 4:00, it might help me regain some memories. At least it might start getting me better."

"That's how they explained it to me. Well, I'm all in! And for the record, I love France and everything related to the French. That's one of my favorite hobbies, I guess. Anyway, I hope it works."

They actually smiled at each other as they started to talk about the delicious choices of tea, coffee, and every type of culinary delight they could imagine. Finger sandwiches, macaroons, and the accompanying pastries.

Mary Beth announced, "I'm going to order a special apricot tea that my sister and I ordered on our first day in Paris. It was heavenly, and they carry it here. Harney & Sons Fine Teas Apricot Tea Fruity, Black Tea"

"Oh, look," said Antonio. "They have a sampler with demi cups of five teas to share. I'm going to order that too. Maybe they'll have something that seems familiar to me."

Their waitress brought their order, and the fun began.

"I haven't had a treat like this since I went to Tahiti earlier this year. Since that's French Polynesia, the resort offered French food and pastries."

"Wow! I wonder if I've ever been there. Only time will tell."

"Antonio, it's an island country in the Pacific Ocean, and you would love it. You should keep a notebook of stuff you hear about. When you regain your memory, you can look at them in a few days."

After they finished their High Tea excursion, they headed out to explore the village.

Mary Beth kept an eye on Antonio as they strolled down the sidewalk. *"After all, I was told that walking might jog his memory and be good for him. The amnesia doctor asked us to relax and be open to the fact that it might trigger something that would bring up memories. Hopefully, this will start getting his mind working along those lines."*

As they lingered at the shop windows, making small talk, each concentrated on what was of interest to them. Antonio was looking across the street and lagging behind when something else caught Mary Beth's attention.

She couldn't resist the sweet aroma and beauty of an old-fashioned flower cart parked in front of the Florist Shop. It was overflowing with a colorful array of spectacular summer blossoms. This floral treasure was a prime distraction from what was parked nearby. One look at the beautiful blue hydrangeas and Mary Beth was hooked. As she approached the cart, she was in awe of the simple joy that this display brought her. *"This is absolutely beautiful. It truly fills my soul with happiness."*

She had no idea she had ignored a black hearse strangely parked on the side of the street. Seated inside, Jack and the other smugglers were watching her every move. "What are we planning to do," asked Charlie as they watched Mary Beth.

"I'm not sure, but whatever it is, this might be our golden opportunity," replied Jack. After a second, he continued, "I feel several other people are watching them also. It looks like maybe it's an undercover team assuring their safety. We need to think of something quick, or we'll miss the opportunity."

Across the street, Antonio wandered into a tattoo shop. The owner, who hadn't had a customer all day, asked, "What do you like?"

He responded, "I don't know what I like right now!"

"Well, what are some of your favorite or happiest times? Or hobbies?"

Antonio was in awe of the vast painted walls, mainly with motorcycle art. Then he glanced up and was amazed again by the continued art on the ceiling. "Well, the only thing that comes to mind is... I like Zorro and... I like dancing," he added quickly.

"Do you have any other tattoos?"

"Not that I know of," Antonio answered as he wondered if he was lucky enough to have any of these wonderful images.

"Well, sit down," the delighted artist invited. "Since this is your first time, I'll give you half-off."

Antonio was so involved with the art that all he heard was, "Blah, blah, blah... this will hurt for a second."

The tattoo artist took the sharp instrument and touched Antonio's shoulder muscle. He let out a blood-curdling scream, "Ouch! Hey! What are you doing?"

Mary Beth heard the cry and ran into the tattoo shop, yelling, "What's going on here? Stop!"

"I'm getting a tattoo, but he said it wouldn't hurt!" Antonio lamented angrily.

Meanwhile, this was just the lucky break the smugglers needed. "Larry, here, duck into that costume shop around the corner and pick up the things on this list. Make it fast! That lady just ran into the tattoo place, and that distraction won't last long."

Mary Beth immediately took Antonio's hand and indignantly yanked him out of the chair. "Come on, we're getting out of here!" Then she reprimanded him with frustration when she looked at his wounded arm, "Well, you'll have to get that removed!"

After they were back on the street, she continued in a calmer voice, "I think it's time to get back to the hospital. The doctor wants to discuss whether this helped with your memory loss."

She led him briskly along the fairytale street toward the medical center.

Antonio dejectedly said, "In my defense, they said I'd get it half off. I liked that, and they promised I could get a tattoo of something I wanted. I found out I like Zorro. Do you think I'm just remembering from my childhood?

"Maybe," Mary Beth replied thoughtfully. "Although everybody likes Zorro! Do you think you dressed up like Zorro for Halloween?"

"I don't remember anything about Halloween." After a short pause, he continued sadly, "What is it?"

"It's a holiday we celebrate here in America. The children dress up in a costume and go door-to-door to receive candy and treats."

"That sounds like fun," he responded happily. "That's the first thing I'll ask the medical team. Does France celebrate Halloween?"

Mary Beth explained, "I'm pretty sure most French people do not celebrate it as Americans do. For instance, if you want scary in Paris, the first place to head is the infamous Paris Catacombs. This underground cemetery holds more than six million remains in its network of tunnels. However, you probably want to party more in keeping with America's style. In that case, Disneyland Paris hosts an annual Halloween festival for several weeks in the fall."

Then she added hopefully, as they approached and entered the first set of double doors of the Coast Guard Medical Center, "Do you think this helped regain any of your memory?"

"I'm not sure, but the tastes and décor of the café were wonderful. The village was picturesque, and I enjoyed your company."

Two police officers were stationed at a second set of doors. They opened the doors for a laundry cart to exit the building and signaled Antonio to proceed inside.

Antonio continued his appraisal of their delightful afternoon, "Well, I sure won't need any supper this evening. That was a delicious layout of teas and pastries we had, wasn't it?"

This was met with dead silence!

He stopped and turned around to find they had all vanished into thin air, along with the laundry cart!

Chapter Eighteen

Antonio started yelling, "Mary Beth!! Help!! Somebody Help!!" as the actual security guards came running.

"Mary Beth was just with me walking through this door, and now she's vanished. The two policemen and the guy pushing the laundry cart are all gone."

The Coast Guard Medical Center and grounds went on high alert and lock down mode.

However, the black funeral vehicle was long gone. A lone, over-turned laundry cart was discovered in the ditch. A faint scent of Chanel would be detected under careful police analysis.

It turned out that Mary Beth was not the ideal kidnapping candidate that they had expected. They had given her a small amount of chloroform to knock her out. This had a minimal effect on her, but it was enough to make her go limp so they could dump her into the cart. While they had tried to transport her in the laundry cart to the hearse, she woke up and tried to climb out.

Jack was livid, "Hey, you guys! Stop her! Don't let her get out!"

Charley yelled, "I'm trying," as he tried to shove her back in while he grabbed the smelling salts that he'd picked up by mistake. She almost got the rest of the way out of the cart this time.

"What are you doing?" Jack cried, "I don't believe you guys! Are those your grandmother's 'smelling salts'? I told you yesterday those are not the same as knockout drops! You're making it worse!"

"Well, I didn't have my reading glasses, and I thought it said inhalers, not smelling salts. I'm not up on all this stuff!"

"Where do you think we'd be able to get your fancy morphine or chloroform, anyway?"

Bill jumped in with, "Hey, give me those handcuffs!" As he tried to put them on her, he got a big surprise. Mary Beth wasn't cooperating with that plan either, as she broke the toy handcuffs.

Jack was fed up with their stupid antics, "Oh no! Are those the handcuffs from the costume store?"

Bill answered, "What did you think we had?"

"You guys are all idiots!"

After a free-for-all, they finally got Mary Beth into the hearse, just in time to avoid the police cars that flew by, looking for the kidnappers.

"Use your handkerchiefs to shut her up, quiet her down, and tie her up! This is not good!"

"This fighting has got to stop! Keep her under control back there," Jack yelled as the hearse finally quit fishtailing from side to side.

Within minutes, the hearse skidded around the corner and drove directly into the sunset!

Chapter Nineteen

Over the next few minutes, Jack argued with the other two geniuses about their demands. "Listen, when we talk to the authorities on the burner phone, we must have clear demands. We don't know if the guy even discovered gold or treasure near those newly exposed railroad tracks."

Soon, the hearse pulled into a parking spot by an old building with apartments on the top floor. They got out and dragged Mary Beth to their rented condo above the store-fronts. They tied her hands behind her back (Big Mistake) and slammed the door. Jack turned to his team, "Now let's figure out our demands so we can place the call. Then, let's try to get some sleep."

"Well," said Charlie. "Why don't we just give this 'dame' back. She's a lot more trouble than I thought she'd be."

Bill agreed, "Yeah, she's unbelievably strong for a lady! I never imagined that putting up with the likes of her would be so difficult! However, ...I sure didn't sign up for murder!"

"No," insisted Jack! "We aren't actually going to hurt her. She's just collateral, so we can get the gold."

Bill breathed a sigh of relief. "I'm glad to hear it since we don't have a gun, and none of us know how to use it if we did."

Jack was unhappy with his remarks, "Well, they don't know that. Just for the record, you two are terrible at this line of work!"

"Well, excuse me!" justified Bill. "I just need the treasure to help pay my mom's medical bills."

Jack agreed, "We each have overdue urgent needs, speaking of which, I'm going to lose my house, for heaven's sake. We need to find something legal to keep whatever gold that guy found. How about we get a clear title and rights to all those newly exposed railroad cars and tracks? Both above and below the land."

That's when their tied-up hostage re-entered their nightmare. "Hey, boys! I've got a marvelous idea!"

Jack's head snapped in surprise, "I thought you gagged her!"

"Never mind that," she bragged. "I know all kinds of self-defense moves. In fact, I teach a course in high school to help girls get out of any trouble you guys could think up. I also teach the same tactics to women two weekends a month."

"You're kidding! Just shut up! You're our hostage!"

"Well, you'll need my help to get out of this mess alive," she warned matter-of-factly.

Charlie jumped in, "Hey Boss, let her talk. We've got nothing to lose."

"Well, first, let's clarify the ground rules before I help you out," she said flippantly as she tossed their rope in the air.

"You're nuts!" declared Jack. "There are no ground rules on your side."

"That's your choice, but in all fairness and legally, in the interest of full disclosure, I feel I must let you know what my summer job was during my college years. You'll each get one guess!"

"Hey, we're not going to play foolish guessing games with you," Jack fumed.

Mary Beth shrugged her shoulders, with a 'who cares' attitude, "Well, excuse me! I was just trying to even the playing field! However, as a trained professional, I must ask, do you guys know anything about the martial arts? You know judo, karate?"

"What are you planning to do to us?" asked Jack.

Mary Beth calmly asked, "Have you guys ever seen someone win at Mah Jongg? It will test even the best of us, but I'm very good at it. I've won several Mah Jongg Tournaments. In fact, I was supposed to practice later today." She cracked her knuckles and said, "I know. I wouldn't mind practicing right now. There's no referee around, so I could go wild!"

Before this got any worse, Charlie interrupted, "Hey, never mind that. I'm ready to try a guess! Okay, I guess you were an intern at an attorney's office."

Mary Beth paused thoughtfully for pure drama, "That's a great answer. However, It's dead wrong!" She said, "Strike one!" with an ominous smile. "With every wrong answer, I get to ask you a question, and you need to tell me the truth, or I'm out!"

"What?"

"I'll now ask you a question, and if I find out you lied, I'll refuse to help you get any gold!"

"Now, I have their attention with some added leverage. Let's see who will actually give me a truthful answer. Meanwhile, I wish Maggie and the FBI would hurry up. I don't know how long I can stall these clowns."

"Okay, Charlie, you gave the wrong answer; I'll ask you the question. How did you learn about the gold, and how much do you think is left?"

"Don't answer!" yelled Jack.

After a moment of hesitation, Charlie looked at the floor and waivered. "I better not say!"

"Perfect! I see that neither Jack nor Charlie wants to be spared the wrath of the entire FBI Secret Service! That's rich," she laughed. "Out of the goodness of my heart, I'll give you a free piece of advice: My best friend is FBI Special Agent Maggie O'Hara-Jensen. If anything happens to me, she will not be handing out any 'Get out of Jail Free' cards to either of you two."

"Okay," Charlie practically screamed, "I see no harm in explaining what we've heard."

"Well, then, let's have it! And it better be the truth!" She stated seriously.

"Since we were kids, we've heard about the Legend of the Lost Civil War Gold. We even dug up a few spots as teenagers, hoping to find gold. Of course, we only found a few arrowheads, bullets, and other historical stuff of little or no value.

"The Legend all started in 1863 before the Battle of Gettysburg. It claims that the Union Army shipped a wagon train filled with gold South to pay Union soldiers. The transport departed from Wheeling, West Virginia, as planned. However, when it arrived at St. Mary's, Pennsylvania, the shipment of gold had disappeared."

Jack agreed, "We have lived through the decades of rumors that the story was fictional. However, it has persisted for generations. Meanwhile, there have been various searches over the years with no gold bullion found. Even the FBI has dug on Dent's Run, PA state land, and carried off something secret to an undisclosed area. Big surprise, now its records are all sealed in Washington D.C."

Charlie recalled the story again, "A man who owns a Finders Keepers recovery service has been searching for decades also. He still believes it's in that vicinity but has not found it.

"But most of the theories about the gold have been met with skepticism from state officials and local historians. One of the treasure hunters who searched for the lost gold even hired a private investigator to comb through government records in Washington, D.C. He also came up empty. His last statement was, 'We found no credible evidence that there was ever gold there.' That's why we're interested in seeing if gold was by those abandoned railroad tracks."

No one talked for a minute or two.

Mary Beth made another stab at delaying their kidnapping plans. "Very good, Charlie and Jack. That's a very believable motivation, and I believe you."

"I'm almost ready to help you guys with a path to survival. Does anyone else want to earn my goodwill by offering an answer for my summer job during college?"

Bill asked, "Could you give us a clue?"

Mary Beth slowly got up from the chair, but no one tried to stop her. "Now let me see. If you trust me, I can give you an example of what I did."

She was quiet and non-threatening as she turned to stand behind the chair and calmly looked into each of their eyes. *"I do not see killers, but everyday people who have their backs against the wall and have gotten over their heads in pursuing treasure."*

"Do you trust me?"

"Well, I doubt you could hurt us in any way, so what do we have to lose," remarked Bill.

"I promise not to hurt any of you while I show you a clue. Are we all in agreement?"

They all nodded their heads, sealing the bargain.

With a totally inappropriate smile, she removed the handcuffs from her pocket and spread her arms. She slowly walked behind Jack and said, "Do you trust me?"

He almost laughed as he jeered, "Of course, you already proved those are a child's toy!"

"I know, but please humor me and put your hands behind your back just for effect." She chucked.

He thought, *"why not humor her with this stupid trick?"* As he put his hands behind his back, Mary Beth quickly cuffed and clicked them with an innocent smile.

"All right, I know what you did for your job," cried Charlie joyfully. "You were a magician's assistant."

Mary Beth threw open her arms and said, "Yes, It's Show-time!"

They all clapped their hands except Jack, who struggled to remove the cuffs. At last, he gave up, "Get these off me!"

Mary Beth smiled as she said, "Now I'm going to prove something to you. You trusted me to let me put these on one of you; now You can try to get them off Jack's wrist. However, I guarantee that it won't work. Because of a Magician's oath that I took, I cannot reveal how I do it, but I will certainly remove them for you, Jack."

She stepped behind him and removed them with a few clicks, like the combination of a lock on a vault. She stepped out in front of them with the handcuffs dangling from her hands and took a bow.

"Now, I believe you guys have big financial problems and thought you had an answer. Then you got treasure fever, and you got carried away. Have you been in trouble before this whole series of events?" As they shook their heads no, she continued, "Then, let's begin to get this whole situation resolved."

Chapter Twenty

During the previous hour, Maggie repeatedly questioned why we hadn't gotten any demands from the kidnappers of Mary Beth. *"This is not good!"*

She called the FBI team to hear of any progress they may have made with the kidnapping. "We don't have any leads yet? Did you see anything strange on the camera footage, pulling away from the Coast Guard Medical Center?"

"The cameras were tracking the arrival of the incoming Search and Rescue Helicopter. It was arriving with two surfers who had been carried out to sea and suffered exhaustion trying to return to the beach. The cameras weren't pointed towards the front doors at the time of the kidnapping."

"Okay, I'm going to cruise the area up here by the Coast Guard Medical Center and proceed toward the village. I'm looking for anything that looks out of place. So far, we've got nothing!"

As Maggie surveyed the entrance road approaching the front doors of the medical center, she couldn't help but view all the shrubs and extensive landscaping. *"That holds numerous places to hide a vehicle that was lying in wait. Wow, how much of the kidnapping area would the cameras be able to film?"*

She continued to travel down the various roads that were probably used to escape undetected by the authorities. She researched an outlying area with a mix of less expensive stores and apartments. She didn't see the lampposts with hanging baskets or the picturesque design that was evident in the lovely area of the village. *"I need to check out this whole area."*

A half-hour later, Maggie spotted a vehicle with a suspicious license plate, TTY 1023. *"What is that license plate doing on a hearse? Vehicles that start with the capital 'T' are only designated for trucks in this state."*

She slowed down, made a U-Turn, and pulled over a couple of parking spaces away.

Maggie called the FBI database operator. "Hello, this is FBI Special Agent Maggie O'Hara-Jensen. Could you please check the license plate number TTY 1023?"

The operator asked, "Sure. Did you want this sent to your headquarters, or are you waiting for it?"

"Both; I've got a visual on the vehicle now. Something's not right about it, and the plates are attached to a hearse of all things."

"Oh, yes, I've got something in that. Here we go. A hearse was reported stolen by a funeral director this afternoon. They assume it was 'borrowed' by one of the part-time employees named Jack. Someone remembers seeing him driving it this morning but assumed he was filling the gas tank. He worked on and off as they needed him. However, Jack spends most of his time as a beachcomber."

"Okay," replied Maggie. "I'll take a look." She exited her car and carefully moved toward the hearse with her gun drawn.

The hearse appeared vacant, so she had a chance to look it over well. The back area was curtained, but she saw something special when she looked through the rear window. The beautiful charm of the Eiffel Tower lay on the velvet material.

"Bingo! Now we're getting somewhere. I gave Mary Beth that charm bracelet for Christmas last year."

She pulled her mobile phone from her pocket and dialed for backup. As she approached the building, her phone rang. She glanced at the screen and thought, *"That's an unknown number, similar to what I'd expect from a burner phone."* Maggie answered immediately.

"Special Agent Maggie O'Hara-Jensen"

"Maggie, It's Mary Beth. I'm fine."

"What? I just found your gold Eiffel Tower charm from your Christmas bracelet in the hearse."

"Yes, I left it for a little clue for you."

"Well, backup is on the way."

"No, you don't need them. We're upstairs above the stores. These three men are officially giving themselves up. I figured you'd be looking for me. The guys I was with were ready to give themselves up for the assault on Antonio. They thought he was going to steal their gold claim. They'd never been in trouble before and certainly didn't mean to strike him so hard. They panicked after they realized that he was really hurt."

"What are you talking about? These men kidnapped you, and they will pay for it!"

"Oh, Maggie, I'm fine! And please don't come in with guns blazing! You'll really scare them!"

Chapter Twenty-One

As Maggie ran up the stairs to the condo above the stores, Mary Beth ran out to meet her.

"Maggie! Over here."

"Mary Beth, are you all right?"

"Yes, I told you. I'm fine. Come on in, and I'll explain everything."

As Maggie entered the condo, the three men welcomed her and shook her hand. "Thank you for coming, Ma'am."

Maggie was not precisely thrilled with these kidnappers, and it started with their assault on her long-time friend, Antonio. *"These stellar pillars of the community have caused his memory loss, and I'm not happy."*

Maggie tried to control her anger. "First, I need to call off the FBI backup plan, the swat team, and the sniper. I'll use the special agents to bring the three of you downtown to the FBI headquarters to be interviewed and charged if appropriate."

She didn't take her eyes off these guys as she made her call. "I know, I know. Mary Beth is fine. She assures me these guys have a legitimate reason for everything."

The voice on the other end said, "Boy, this better be good. Our squad will be there in 5 minutes to help you apprehend them and take them to headquarters."

"Wait!" Maggie explained, "Mary Beth made a special request, and I quote, 'Don't come in with guns blazing! You'll scare them!"

They responded with disbelief.

"I know it's ridiculous, but they are completely unarmed."

Mary Beth walked over as Maggie finished her call. "Thank you! Now, one additional favor, and it means a lot to me."

"Okay, I'm so relieved that I'll agree to almost anything."

"Well, my friend. Have you ever had anyone appear to be one thing, and when you got to know them, they turned out to be entirely different?"

"Oh, you mean like the other side of their coin," asked Maggie? *"Wow, I remember what a difference my husband James was from how I first saw him. Yes, we both misjudged each other the entire time we were falling in love!"*

"Yes, only they were not who you thought they were. In fact, you may be asking these men for their help before the day is through. On my behalf, please don't use handcuffs on these men when you 'invite' them down to the FBI headquarters."

Maggie's mouth dropped open as she looked over at these men. "Mary Beth, I'll do as you ask, but that's because I trust you. After all, they are unarmed, and you must have heard something incredible from them." She continued her thoughts: *"I have a feeling you don't plan to press kidnapping charges either, my dear friend. I'm famous for figuring out suspects, but I don't know about this one."*

There were no guns or handcuffs involved in their exit from the hideout. On the way down to the headquarters, no sirens were heard from any vehicles involved. The FBI dropped the lone hearse with a full gas tank at the funeral parlor. No questions asked.

Chapter Twenty-Two

Meanwhile, back at the medical center, Doctor Lewis paid a visit to Antonio to break the good news about the release of Mary Beth.

"Hello, Antonio," the doctor smiled as he entered the room. "We have wonderful news about Mary Beth. She's free, and she's fine."

"Wow, how did that happen?"

The doctor continued, "Well, it's almost a miracle. However, the kidnappers have turned themselves in. I'm dying to hear all the details, but in all my time at the medical center, I've never heard of anything like this happening."

"What do you mean?"

"Well, FBI Special Agent Maggie, whom they claim was a very close friend of yours, is interviewing them right now."

"Where? At their hideout? And how do we know Mary Beth is all right?"

"Slow down, Antonio. I don't know any answers, but they are recording the interview, so we can view it later." He stopped abruptly and regarded him, stalling and evaluating if he should continue.

Antonio asked curiously, "Okay, what are you NOT telling me?"

"Well, there is one outstanding unbelievable part that none of us understand yet."

"I'm pretty sure it's not the most shocking thing I've heard over the past 24 hours, so go ahead and tell me."

"Okay, but I can't explain it myself," he paused, trying to figure out if he should. After a moment, he proceeded, "Here is the thing. Neither one of us knows Mary Beth, right?"

Antonio nodded, "I'm trying to get to know her. Granted, I wasn't too sure about her when I first met her, and I thought she'd hit me with something to knock me out. But now I've learned she probably saved my life by interrupting the smugglers' attack. Plus, she apparently bandaged my head, which you said was good. I like how she smells, but she doesn't look familiar to me."

The doctor asked, "How did it go today, when you two met for 'High Tea,' up to the time of the kidnapping? Did she seem 'normal' to you?"

Antonio just stared at him suspiciously. "Well, come to think of it, she got awfully upset about me trying to get a tattoo. The artist was promising me a half-off deal for a Zorro tattoo. He just started, and it really hurt. When I yelled, Mary Beth came running in and yelled at both of us. She even yanked me out of the chair and said I'd have to get that removed. She's not my mother!"

The doctor almost laughed at that, but he controlled himself as he continued. "Some of her actions don't seem logical, and I can't find their motivation. She seems very protective of you. However, she refuses to file any charges for her kidnapping. In fact, she ordered a wonderful lunch for them to eat during the interview. I can't for the life of me figure her out."

Chapter Twenty-Three

Meanwhile, back at the FBI Headquarters, this had turned into one of the strangest investigations Maggie had ever been in charge of. She directed the men into a conference room and asked them to be seated.

"Would you like something to drink? Mary Beth ordered a tray of hamburgers and fries with all the fixings. They should be here as soon as the microphone and video are set up."

"That would be very kind of you, Ma'am," said Jack.

"I think I'd like Yoo-hoo if you have it, but don't open it," stated Charlie as he looked down at the table.

"Or any kind of soda would be okay. Whatever you have is fine," added Bill.

Just then, Mary Beth entered, leading a couple of servers from the kitchen carrying platters laden with hamburgers, French fries, coleslaw, potato salad, and all the fixings.

The last thing she took from under the tray's shelf was a case of cold Yoo-hoo. She slid the box beside Charlie's chair and whispered, "This is for your little boy!"

Well, Maggie was floored, to say the least. *"Who were these men?"*

After a few minutes, Maggie finished setting everything up. The men were busy eating, so she thought she'd give them an outline of what she would ask them about.

"Hello, I'm FBI Special Agent Maggie O'Hara-Jensen.

"With your permission, I will ask you some questions about the last few days. I have no idea what you've told Mary Beth. However, it must be incredible. She has complete trust in each of you, which I find phenomenal, and to be quite frank, I find it downright unbelievable after what we thought was an assault and kidnapping."

She paused before she continued. "She is one of my dearest friends, and I also trust her implicitly. With that in mind, I'd like to know what you've seen and heard over the last 48 hours. I'm ready to be equally amazed, so please tell me what you told Mary Beth when you're ready."

"Yes," said Jack. "I'll start, and we can each tell our memory as we go along if that works."

"Of course, that would be very helpful!" answered Maggie. "Since this is just a 'fact-finding interview,' Mary Beth, you may join us if you'd like."

Jack looked at Bill and Charlie, and they all nodded their agreement.

After Mary Beth poured a cup of coffee, she sat at the large mahogany conference table.

Jack started, "I guess what would be pertinent to these proceedings started a couple of days ago. The three of us have been friends since childhood. We have always been interested in treasure hunting, gold, etc. As teenagers, we heard about the Legend of the Lost Civil War Gold Shipment. It intrigued us; we even dug several places where we thought we might discover it."

Bill added, "We are also interested in over 2,000 old abandoned railroad tracks that crisscross the United States. We knew several tracks were lost during hurricanes and storms that buried them under tons of debris. At times, the water of rivers and streams were permanently diverted."

Jack picked it up, "when the last hurricane uncovered the railroad tracks and many buried rail cars along the nearby coast, we were excited. We took a boat out, and over the previous week or so, we searched along the banks for anything valuable. We saw the newly exposed railroad tracks and investigated further. We thought we could secure the rights to anything of value we found if we dug something up, so we filed a claim on that property and the mineral rights under the surface.

"The next day, we were approaching the abandoned railroad tracks in our boat when we met another boat containing real smugglers interested in using the newly opened area for drug drops."

Maggie broke in, "Okay, now you've got my attention. What happened?"

"We saw a boat following close to us, with one man steering the boat and two other guys lying flat on the bottom of the vessel like they were hiding. We saw multiple bags of something wrapped in plastic and seaweed being dragged behind. We immediately thought they were smugglers with drugs hanging off the back of their boats. They were heavily armed and dangerous and didn't want anyone interfering with their drug business. They claimed it was their territory and warned us at gunpoint to leave the area.

"We didn't disclose our pending claim on the exposed railroad cars and tracks. We haven't had any of this approved yet. We don't own any type of guns and weren't prepared to fight them on any level."

Bill added, "To explain our situation further, our families have each fallen on hard times. My mom has many unpaid medical bills, and her health is very bad.

"Charlie lost his job when the local businesses folded up or closed their doors due to the economy. He can't even afford to buy Yoo-hoo for his little boy. That kind of thing is hard to deal with. We have no employment opportunities in our little town.

"Jack's home is in foreclosure. He can't find work. His family is ready to lose their home and has no options left to try.

"None of us seem to be able to find extra work. We thought we had a shot in these uncovered railroad tracks. We were desperate to get money honestly for our bills. We were not trying to steal anything.

"When we saw the man we hit on the head with the driftwood, we assumed he was looking for the drug drop, and we followed him into the abandoned rail car. Now, he was interfering with our gold claim.

"When we heard someone else approaching, we hit Antonio over the head with a piece of driftwood. Just to give us time to escape unnoticed. We thought they were coming with their guns. We wanted to get away before they came around that corner.

"We hid behind some cliff rocks and were shocked when a lady showed up with a clipboard. We did feel terrible that we hurt him so badly. We aren't killers. We thought he was one of the armed and dangerous drug dealers. We also thought the lady must be part of the gang.

"The next thing we knew, the Search and Rescue helicopter was landing near the railroad tracks and hauling the drug drop guy away. The drug lady went in the helicopter also.

"It didn't look like it was headed to Sea Crest, so we figured it was headed to the Coast Guard Medical Center.

"We assumed at least the guy would be arrested. We thought they were part of the drug operation.

"We hoped to get ahold of the lady to see if they were arrested."

Maggie stopped them right there. "Do you think you could identify the real drug dealers?"

Jack, Charley, and Bill all nodded their heads in unison. "Yes," said Jack. "We don't want these drug dealers anywhere near our families. We'd gladly help in any way possible to stop them from getting a foothold in our community!"

Chapter Twenty-Four

Mary Beth pulled Maggie aside, "I need to talk with you for a minute."

Maggie had a good idea of what was on her mind as she joined her with their backs to the guys. She cleared her throat and asked Mary Beth, "Do you have something to add to their story?"

Mary Beth quietly whispered, "Maggie, after everything that happened, I can't in good conscience file charges for kidnapping. I think their motive was good. They've had real-life hardships to deal with and were trying to make an honest living. As for Antonio, they didn't mean to hit an innocent man. They were trying to save their gold claim from the smugglers and thought the intruder would be armed and dangerous at best."

Maggie said, "Are you through?"

"Well, not really. We need to explain the situation to Antonio. I'm sure he'd understand if he knew their motivation was really self-defense against what they thought were smugglers armed to the hilt. After all, he's like an international drug policeman.

"I think we could present their case, and they have offered help with the ID of some real drug smugglers. I think that fact should be accepted in exchange for leniency for the assault on Antonio. After all, they thought Antonio was a drug smuggler."

Maggie agreed, "I'll have to see what we can work out, but you had me at, 'Maggie, I need to talk to you.' I can read you like a book."

Mary Beth smiled, "You're the one who always believes in second chances. Plus, you know we shouldn't take advantage of a situation just because you can. A very wise, generous person once told me, 'Just because you have the right to do something, doesn't mean it's the right thing to do.'"

"Okay," Maggie protested. "I'll see what I can do."

"Great, I know they live the next town over from Sea Crest, but I think they could all use a good-paying job. Possibly at the new Sea Crest Museum? They also know a lot of local history about what happened in this area."

"You're right," stated Maggie.

Maggie turned to address the three men who were nervously waiting. "Mary Beth was right. I am pleased to say that I am also incredibly pleased to ask for your help with our smuggling problems."

Jack stepped forward and stated, "Yes, we are prepared to help ID and work in any way we can to redeem ourselves, to clear our names."

Maggie said, "Your good friend Mary Beth has refused to file kidnapping charges against you. I agree that that's the right thing to do under the circumstances."

"We will explain this situation to the gentleman hit with the driftwood. I'd say it was a case of self-defense and/or mistaken identity against the real smugglers and the fear of them stealing your gold claim. Of course, he's within his rights to file assault charges, but I doubt that will happen after Mary

Beth and I share what happened with him. Either way, I would like to go ahead with your help to catch the smugglers."

As they picked up their stuff, she said, "Mary Beth and I need to say goodbye. We'll be in touch."

Chapter Twenty-Five

Maggie and Mary Beth arrived at the Coast Guard Medical Center shortly. "Can you believe Antonio was trying to get a tattoo?" Mary Beth said.

"Well, he doesn't know who he is and why that might not be the best idea," explained Maggie.

"I feel responsible. I was supposed to be helping him regain his memory, and I was distracted by the beautiful flower cart. I mean, that village is simply charming."

"By the way, is there a ladies' lounge where I could wash up and run a comb through my hair? I don't want to look like I've been roughed up or harmed in any way by my kidnapping adventure."

"Oh, Mary Beth!" Maggie laughed, "You're something else. Let's see if Kate is in her office. She often has to change from her pilot uniform to her Coast Guard uniform or street clothes. She keeps a few extra sets of clothes here."

They knocked on her door, and Kate waved them in and greeted them with open arms. "Wow, talk about excitement. I'm so glad you're safe, Mary Beth!"

"I'm fine!" she said. "We're on our way to see Antonio, and I thought I should freshen up. I don't want to look like I've been hurt or roughed up."

"Good idea. Come on in. I've been wondering how the whole interview with the smugglers came out!"

"Well, the whole day was full of surprises. Do you want to join us when we talk with Antonio? I will share some of it at our Mah Jongg meeting tomorrow morning. We have a couple of new 'Anonymous Acts of Kindness' to plan and deliver. The sooner, the better."

"Sounds good," replied Kate. She picked up the phone and ordered coffee, tea, a fruit platter, and an assortment of various pastries for the room.

Mary Beth was finishing up her makeover when Maggie had an idea. *"Let's see if Antonio reacts to his Chanel N°5 memory."*

Maggie casually said, "Hey, Mary Beth, do you have any of that wonderful Chanel *N°5* Mist? It's such a light and special scent."

"Yes, good idea. I carry a tiny spray test bottle of it in my purse. It always makes me feel lovely."

Minutes later, Maggie, Kate, and Mary Beth met Antonio in one of the private meeting rooms of the Medical Center. The food and drinks had been set up, and everything looked scrumptious.

Antonio immediately left his seat at the table. As he approached her, he exclaimed with a worried, "Mary Beth, are you all right?"

She smiled and said, "Yes, I'm fine!"

He finished his last step towards her and opened his arms to hug her. Her familiar scent reached his memory, and he held her lightly for a second before the flash of a precious dancer flooded his mind and heart. He stumbled and momentarily caught both of them in an embrace before falling into the chair together.

Antonio mumbled in alarm, "Désolé ma chère!" (So sorry, my friend!) in complete confusion. As they tried to fumble out of the chair, he felt confused and uncertain about what was happening.

Mary Beth knew he didn't mean for them to end up in a heap in the chair, so she gently said, "It's okay. It's okay." She tried to gently extricate herself from the chair. At last, they could separate, and now each sat exhausted and mortified their own chairs.

Maggie knew what was happening and asked Mary Beth to get coffee at the display table. She whispered to her, "Wow! He was so emotional and worried that you were kidnapped that seeing you was a shock. Are you all right?"

"Yes," whispered Mary Beth. "I think he's suffered some kind of trauma. Should we call Doctor Lewis?"

"I'll ask," answered Maggie. "Antonio, I just saw Doctor Lewis in the hallway. Would you like me to call him?"

"Yes, that might be a good idea. Again, I'm so sorry, Mary Beth. I don't know what happened to me."

"I'm fine. No worries."

Maggie let herself out and asked at the information desk for them to ask Doctor Lewis to come to the conference room regarding John Doe.

A couple of minutes later, the doctor arrived. Maggie met him outside the door and explained what had happened when Mary Beth put on the Chanel N°5 Mist. "As soon as Antonio smelled the scent, he was shocked. I thought he looked like he was dancing with her for one moment before he embraced Mary Beth to break into a collapse, in which they both ended up in the chair. He also spoke French!"

"Well, that's some breakthrough. Do you think Mary Beth knows what he's reacting to?"

"No, she doesn't have a clue. However, she's very worried about Antonio. She feels responsible that she was distracted by a beautiful flower cart in the road when he wandered into a shop to get a tattoo."

"Let's go in now," said Doctor Lewis. "I'll sit next to him. You try to guide Mary Beth across the table next to you."

They entered the room, and Doctor Lewis acknowledged everyone with a smile. "Hi, Antonio. I'm glad I was here." He then turned to Mary Beth, "How are you doing?"

"Hello, I'm fine. But I'm a little concerned about my friend here," she said with a nod towards Antonio.

"Yeah," said Antonio. "I was thrown off from my game, and I don't know what happened to me, but I couldn't control myself. I wanted to hug her and make sure she was really okay. Instead, I started falling and couldn't get my balance. I seemed to lose control and tried to keep her from falling on the floor. I just dragged her down in the chair on top of me. It was really messed up. I'm so sorry, Mary Beth."

"I'm fine. Truly I am," promised Mary Beth.

"Well," Doctor Lewis stated, "I want to put your mind at ease. His memory recovery will sometimes be a little bumpy, which may seem unsettling and strange. The reason is trying to come back and grasp bits and pieces that may not be related at all. It may represent something happy and make your body mirror the moves or actions that go along with that flash of something. It may cause excitement or joy that belongs to that activity. The mind tries to make logic from everything and recover your memories.

"Is it all right if I sit in on your meeting? I assume it's about the smugglers who hit Antonio and kidnapped Mary Beth."

Maggie looked at Antonio and Mary Beth. They each gave their permission.

Maggie started, "This has been one of the strangest cases I've ever encountered. The people and the events did not begin with how we figured them out. We have the facts to prove what we should do under these circumstances. We also have some vital people to help identify one of the most enormous drug rings we've ever run up against.

"I'll show you the interview, then discuss where we stand with taking them down."

With that, Maggie started the video.

After the video finished, Maggie said, "I think we can all agree, watching that whole thing was like watching an onion being peeled. Start with what you think happened, who the smugglers were, and then the real smugglers were revealed. You thought you knew who hit Antonio and why he was hit. Then you hear about what was happening during the assault. The who, why, and where it happened turned upside down."

Kate added, "That fits what I observed when our SARS team arrived in response to Mary Beth's 911 call."

Maggie nodded yes, as she continued, "By the end of their interview, I heard your comments of, 'Wow, I never saw that coming,' 'I didn't know that,' and 'You're kidding me.'"

"As for the kidnapping of our dear friend, Mary Beth, she recognized that these men had no kidnapping skills. They constantly used their real names in front of her, and they had no weapons. The more she heard and saw them, the more she believed they weren't smugglers at all. They were trying to protect their gold claim from a ruthless drug ring that had threatened them at gunpoint.

"Mary Beth was not afraid of them, but she uncovered the true heart of these men. Turning them into heroes with families and problems bigger than they knew how to solve. Yes, they are more than willing to identify the true smugglers.

"What a shocking turn of events, to be sure. However, as you can probably guess, Mary Beth cannot, in full conscience, press charges in this case. She single-handedly brought the answers to fixing the problem while giving those families a second chance. Hopefully, their luck will not be stacked against them as they progress.

"Now, as for you, Antonio, in light of this new information, I do not know how you feel about your terrible assault. You are certainly within your rights to file charges. You've lost your memory, and that's totally unfair. I don't know if understanding that these guys had mistaken you for someone heavily armed who'd threatened their lives makes any difference to you. It won't return your memory any faster, either way.

"However, we're going to take them up on their offer to identify the real smugglers and help us stop this huge drug ring that is forming here at Sea Crest. They understand they are not off the hook for hitting you with the driftwood. Your back was to them, so they thought you were one of the smugglers who had warned them to stay away from this area. To make matters worse, they heard someone else coming. In the interest of self-defense, since they were unarmed, they picked up whatever was handy and used it to give them time to escape safely.

"The bottom line is, if you choose to bring assault charges, they will pay whatever the law dictates. However, the judge will consider their self-defense motive and rule by balancing their willingness to identify the real smugglers against the penalty for assaulting you. They thought their lives were in danger."

Antonio whispered a surprising request, "I'd like a word with Mary Beth if that's okay."

"Oh, of course," Mary Beth answered with a heartfelt agreement as she stepped around to his chair.

Doctor Lewis said, "Here, take my seat," as he motioned Kate and Maggie over to the table with the food display.

Mary Beth smiled, but with concern in her voice, she softly asked Antonio, "What can I help you with?"

"I just wanted to be sure they didn't hurt you. I could never forgive them if they harmed you," he sadly confessed.

"No, I wasn't hurt at all. These men meant no harm to me. However, I learned they had real-life problems with no way out. One of the men has his house in foreclosure. Things like that can devastate a man and affect his family for a long time. It's a loss that destroys his credit and ability to recover their good name, and it can haunt them for a whole generation in some cases.

"Another of these men has a mother who is in terrible health. Her unpaid healthcare bills are astronomical, and she has exhausted her options. She is unable to afford a specialist that might be able to heal her or at least give her some specialized help. These are problems that they can't solve.

"The third man lost his job completely when the company closed due to the economy's downturn. He's from outside that beautiful little village we visited. I discovered that another part of that area is very, very poor. It does not have the fancy fairytale shops and tree-lined streets with flower-filled baskets.

"These men are hardworking, honest people who bought a gold claim on the property where the railroad tracks were exposed after the storm. The real smugglers are heavily armed and ruthless thugs who warned them at gunpoint to stay away from the area."

"Wow, that must have been scary."

"Yes! In fact, I told Maggie that I was fine. Please come meet with us because they wanted to turn themselves in. And please don't come in with 'guns blazing.' It would scare them."

"What did she think of that," he asked.

"She's known me forever. She said she didn't understand but honored my wishes because she trusted me."

Antonio thought about that carefully and then said, "Well, Mary Beth, I haven't known you hardly at all, and I'm not sure about many things, but I feel the same way. I trust you."

He signaled the other guys, "I'm ready to tell you what I've decided to do."

They all joined Antonio at the conference table as he stated, "I'm trying to do the right thing here, and I think I've come up with the right answer. Based on people I trust and care about, I need to trust them more than I can remember. I don't have the memory or skills to develop a plausible answer, but I know and genuinely feel that you're on the right track of the intent of the guys who whacked me. They were scared and unarmed, and their experience had a memory of grabbing the nearest thing to hit me with so they could escape. I think that was very wise and the only defense they saw under the circumstances."

Maggie, Kate, and Doctor Lewis were intently listening. Mary Beth held her breath. *"Please do the unthinkable, Antonio. Don't press assault charges."*

"That being said," Antonio continued. "I will not file assault charges against these men. I wish them the best. Hopefully, I'll be a valuable help in solving the growing drug problem along the Sea Crest Coast, along with them, when I regain my memory. They are doing a brave thing, and I admire them. I don't remember it, but coming up against a drug cartel is very dangerous."

The Doctor added, "I think you could change your mind later when you recover your memory. It seems like a crazy thing to do if someone doesn't know these men's stories. I think you could file charges later if you decide to."

Antonio looked him straight in the eyes as he said firmly, "I won't change my mind unless Mary Beth does."

Chapter Twenty-Six

The following day, the guys showed up for a joint meeting with the DEA operatives working to stop the drug smugglers.

Maggie took the lead in explaining the new attendees. "Good morning! We are joined this morning with some much-needed help by three witnesses to the latest smuggling operation here along the Sea Crest Coastal region. They were also instrumental in identifying known smugglers who have been active in this area. This is Charlie, Bill, and Jack," she finished as the group welcomed them and shook hands.

Next came the confusion of the DEA agents as they recognized the three men as dead ringers for the suspects they were looking for yesterday in the kidnapping case of Mary Beth. "Hey, what's going on?"

"Maggie, they were the kidnappers yesterday!"

"What happened to the charges?"

Maggie said, "Okay, quiet down, everyone. Yesterday's kidnapping was a complete misunderstanding."

"What?" demanded one of the lead agents as he looked confused and frustrated.

Maggie continued, "Well, it was a mistaken identity by all parties involved. Long story short, it was all a big mistake, and the charges were all dropped. In fact, they are the best and only connection to the identity of the real smugglers, and we're fortunate to have their help."

This was met with dead silence as she continued, "Now, let's get down to work and update these men on how we work to catch a smuggler!"

They looked around and followed her lead because Maggie was brilliant and the best Special Agent they'd ever known.

One of the agents stepped up and stated, "Yes. We'll start by bringing them up to speed on the smuggler's transportation of choice. The Scarab Jet Boats are some of the best and fastest. They are built in Cadillac, Michigan; scarabjetboats.com, and they can go over 600 miles per hour."

Another agent took over, "The most effective crafts are called Blue GoBoats, and most are painted a dark shade of blue. Most of their work is done in the dark hours; however, these boats are prepared even if they must travel during the day. The smugglers can pull a blue tarp over the top of the GoBoat and hide everything from air surveillance. It's almost invisible in the blue water.

"These go-fast boats are used for considerable distances, which means they are built to carry large quantities of drugs and fuel. As a result, some go-fast boats are outfitted and used as mobile fuel stations for the smugglers.

"We have a few of these go-boats here that we have confiscated from past drug busts. We used to destroy them. However, that's not the case now. To destroy them is very costly. The engines are rarely damaged, and they can be sold at auction. They can get a great boat for a fraction of the price. However, that also means that we take a chance to sell them right back into the hands of the smugglers. If that happens, we will catch them."

Maggie added, "Luckily, we have the Coast Guard Maritime Operation Center (MOC) just up the coast from Sea Crest. They are working in conjunction with our new FBI undercover operation that we are developing here. We are partnering to keep drugs and weapons from entering our country.

"An example of working together occurred last week. The Coast Guard's radar picked up a slow-moving boat cruising erratically along the coast. Since it was in an area with recent smuggler activity, we were asked to join the effort to intercept it. We planned to approach with our lights out until we were close enough to apprehend them without a lengthy chase. We planned to check for the boat's paperwork and ask about its cargo. We got plenty close and turned on the spot lights and intercom to identify ourselves and ask them to come along side.

"The Coast Guard thought it looked like there were a couple of men hiding in the boat, which had looked suspicious. What we actually found was two sailors fast asleep. The Coast Guard woke them up when they intercepted their boat under armed attack to come aboard. We seized a total of 41 bales of narcotics worth $41 million US dollars. It took five hours to unload and process the drugs. They found various drugs, including heroin, cocaine, opioid fentanyl, and crystal meth.

"This was one of the largest seizures we have been a part of. It would have been terrible if these drugs had entered the Sea Crest community. Even the fact that it was passing through our coastal towns would have attracted many undesirable individuals. We don't want their violent, illegal lifestyle to grow in this area.

"For example, our Sea Crest Police Department usually deals with small-time offenses. That's not to say there is no crime. Still, the Coast Guard Search and Rescue and the Federal Bureau of Investigation had a powerful presence along the coast. The local police had few criminal offenses to deal with. However, infiltrating the community with drug smugglers would destroy their peaceful, healthy lifestyle."

Chapter Twenty-Seven

Jim, one of the DEA agents who had been involved with helping the three men get debriefed and prepared for their new undercover work, took this opportunity to show them some of the latest equipment they'd had access to. "These new infrared binoculars let us see what's happening at night. Of course, that's the most active time for these criminals.

"The cones in your eyes are more sensitive to yellow and red, but the cones barely work in dim light. The rods are more sensitive to the wavelengths of blue and green light. At night, blue-green light will look brighter than red light. So red enables night vision with little impact on others, particularly what you can see."

Charlie picked up a pair and looked through with great excitement. "Wow, this is unbelievable."

Jim explained, "Let's go to the area where we can better watch the sea coast."

They followed him out and along a trail that led toward the water. They settled down and hid in some bushes behind a big tree several hundred years old. They hear some faint crackling in the distance; Bill sets up his binoculars using the side of the tree to stabilize his views and says, "I can see three red beams that are about a hundred yards away, and one too large for the guys that I remember we saw.

As he questions and turns, "What do you think, guys? Is that them?" He looks around and realizes that his buddies are nowhere in sight.

That's when he heard a yell from far away, "Don't run or show any signs of fear. Stand your ground. It's a mother bear and her cubs!"

Chapter Twenty-Eight

When the DEA operatives met the following day, 'The Bears' was one of the first topics they covered. Maggie said, "Let's review some essential safety topics about our area's wildlife. There are a few Bear myths that are actually wrong.

"The first one claims that bears have bad eyesight. That's a common misconception."

Charlie stated, "I've always heard that they have an amazing sense of smell, and that makes up for a lack of vision."

Maggie shook her head and stated, "Well, they actually have excellent eyesight. Bears can see just as well as humans do during the daytime, but it is during the night that their fantastic vision really shines. Bears have amazing night vision like a family's dog or cat."

As they exclaimed their surprise, she continued, "I've asked the Coast Guard Search and Rescue helicopter pilot, Kate Jensen, to join us this morning. She's got first-hand experience and medical education on helping those injured by wildlife in our coastal area."

Kate stepped forward and explained, "Since we have so much beautiful water in the surrounding area, you might think sharks would be a significant threat to us, but you should be even more scared of bears. They attack at much higher rates and can be deadly. This is likely because humans are increasingly imposing on bear habitats. In college, I was involved in a study in Alaska involving Grizzly Bears on Kodiak Island, Alaska.

"Tourists seemed to love getting close-up pictures of the bears, but they should BEWARE! Snapping a great view of a bear catching a salmon in midair with the water rushing by is not worth your life. Grizzly Bear attacks are dangerous.

"Another thing we studied was that not all bears truly hibernate. For instance, Grizzly bears go through a mild form called torpor, in which their heart rate can slow to as low as eight beats per minute. They also do not eat or drink during this time.

"As you know, our community features numerous wild berries. In fact, we have an abundance of sarsaparilla berries, juneberries, cherries, dogwood berries, blueberries, and raspberries. However, we aren't the only consumers of these tasty treats. The bears along our coast are very efficient berry-eaters, consuming up to 30,000 berries daily in a good year. They devour them, stem and all.

"These berries contain antioxidants, and vitamin B-17 is also found in the seeds of some species. Some scientists considered this an anti-cancer compound. The study shows that although cancer occurs in captive bears, it has never been reported in wild bears.

"Another tasty food that bears enjoy is honey. This is another case where the bears eat everything, including the whole hive with bees, honeycombs, and twigs. They will even scoop up bees, bugs, and ants that are in the area. I had always assumed that if a bear climbed a tree to get to the honey, it was cautious to avoid the bees at all costs. I had no idea that they wanted to consume the whole thing!

"This may amaze you regarding the mother bear with her cubs last night. This information is to educate you for your safety. Bears are not all the same.

"One remarkable thing I learned in Alaska was that 'Yes,' the grizzly bears are fiercely protective of their cubs, with about 70% of human deaths as a result. However, among other bears, the results were surprisingly different. Since 1900, the recorded general bear attacks to protect their cubs were almost non-existent."

Kate finished with a smile, "Any questions?"

Jack spoke up, "Thanks for all this information. I've lived in this area my whole life, and although I've lived with the bear population, I've rarely seen one. Of course, I've avoided them, as I did last night."

Kate smiled as she said, "Well, that's the best thing you can do. We do not advise anyone to approach them."

Bill asked, "I have two things. The first is more of a comment. I was pretty surprised that bears were out last night. I also thought they couldn't see as well. Now, I'm doubly aware that they have better night vision than we ever dreamed.

"My question has to do with the fact that you're a search and rescue helicopter pilot. Do you know if bears can swim? Last night, I thought we'd be safe if we could get to the water."

Kate answered, "Yes, bears can swim. I've seen videos of a mother bear with her cubs, visiting a beach and sharing the water for a visit peacefully for a few minutes. Everything seemed to go smoothly, with the people calmly taking a few pictures without creating a dangerous situation.

"I've spoken with some wildlife rangers who said they don't think it's a safe idea to encourage this. It's an increasing problem in some areas, where the humans are encroaching on the shared territory with buildings and highways."

Maggie came forward with closing remarks. “For those new to our growing workforce, we welcome you and appreciate your decision to join us in our mission to end drug smuggling along our coast. Thank you!”

Chapter Twenty-Nine

Doctor Lewis met Mary Beth and Antonio for coffee and suggested, "It might be beneficial to get your memory back quicker if you started to work together on the Scavenger Hunt fundraiser for the Museum."

"Yes, that would be great," agreed Mary Beth. "I want to walk the Sea Crest Church Cemetery. That would be a super place to find questions that need answers for the scavenger hunt contestants."

Antonio said enthusiastically, "Yes, that sounds like a splendid idea!"

Doctor Lewis added, "Grace told me about all the famous and important founders of Sea Crest and its lighthouse, as well as numerous pirates and other interesting historical figures. You should be able to get many things for people to discover as part of the scavenger hunt."

Mary Beth volunteered, "We can use my car. I've got my walking shoes."

"Sounds good. Let's go!"

The good doctor chuckled as he watched them depart, *"I've never seen two people happier to go to a cemetery!"*

Mary Beth asked, "Antonio, what do you remember about the French Rally Scavenger Hunts you were involved in while in Europe?"

He responded, "Well, Doctor Lewis believes that's big on my list of activities that could trigger the return of my memory. I still have lots of notes that I had accumulated to bring to the project. I want to share what I think was the beginning and see if we could incorporate it into our plan."

Mary Beth agreed, "That's a great way to proceed. In fact, I was also gathering information on the day that I found you unconscious. We were both on the same page, although we hadn't even met yet."

Antonio smiled and nodded, "On our way over to the lighthouse, let's talk about a theme or goal of the fund raiser and set up the rules."

When Mary Beth nodded, he continued, "Let's see. We should include various locations and activities where participants would explore the Sea Crest Lighthouse, the coastal areas of interest, the historical Sea Crest Church, and the cemetery. The clues and locations should highlight the exciting history and its local pursuits of charming activities."

"Great! By the way," she added, "I participated in a scavenger hunt as a child growing up; however, this is an important fund raiser and definitely out of my league compared to your experience. I'm unsure of the rules, and we need your expertise to pull it off.

"The rules can be changed and built into the hunt to achieve the best outcome. Our main purpose and goal is to fund the new museum. We must open our teams to 'Matching Funds' of various businesses and clubs. We need to think outside the box on a few non-profits that would love to give us grant money or finance a team."

"I've done some homework on possible grants and funds that may help fund our museum. I ran off a copy for you also, Mary Beth."

She took the folder, looked at the examples, and remarked, "Wow, Antonio! I'm impressed."

"Thanks. I'll give you a brief overview of what I found, and we can get some help approaching these examples and seeing what we can use for our fundraiser.

"The National Parks - "One of the grants that might work is The Maritime Heritage Program, which advances awareness and understanding of the role of maritime affairs in U.S. history. The Grants Program is administered by the National Park Service (NPS) Maritime Heritage Program in partnership with the Maritime Administration (MarAd). The National Maritime Heritage Act (H.R. 3059) became Public Law 103-451 (54 USC 308701-380707). It describes a National Maritime Heritage Policy and establishes the National Maritime Heritage Grants Program within the Department of the Interior.

"The United States Lighthouse Society – Mission Statement- The mission of the United States Lighthouse Society is to preserve and share the history and legacy of America's lighthouses and their keepers. They have some grants that may work for our museum project.

"The Boy and Girl Scouts – The troops can manage a couple of the appropriate stops on the scavenger hunt. They can help the players and stamp their official entry form.

"The Council of American Maritime Museums – Funding opportunity for museums and related organizations across the United States have six opportunities to apply for grants from the Institute of Museum and Library Services (IMLS) in the coming months. This is the nation's primary source of federal funding for museum services."

"Wow," stated Mary Beth. "You've certainly done a splendid job. I have a few realtor friends who are very competent at research. I bet they would volunteer to process these leads for us."

"Okay! Please ask if they'd help us."

Mary Beth pulled up in front of the lighthouse, where they got out. She smiled and announced, "Well, here we are at location #1, The Sea Crest Lighthouse."

Antonio laughed as he explained, "Now you and I get to do the fun part. No one gets a copy of the rules or a copy of the official game until that morning.

"At each stop, we need the players to solve riddles, count bricks or steps, or do anything else we can get them to count to prove they're here. The teams can also complete hilarious photo challenges, look up information in books and pamphlets, or read signs. (One has directions or ID of the next stop.)

"Find the date the Sea Crest Lighthouse was built.

"We give teams #3 tickets to use as they go through the hunt.

"One of the nearby stops can be at the hot dog stand on the beach. Use a riddle like, 'It doesn't bark or snarl, but eating one can be fun. It's plump, sizzles, and fits nicely in a bun.' Answer: A hot dog.

"We give #1 ticket to the 'Snack Shack' vendor on the beach and receive fries. It will buy them one small order of fries and take a picture of each team member eating exactly the same number of fries as is in the team."

Mary Beth added, "Or a picture of an ice cream cone with that number of plastic spoons, and each one gets at least one scoop."

"The team must pick up a sea shell or a small driftwood piece on the beach."

"We could have a pool full of various blow-up toys and playthings. They must find the rubber duck and take a picture with the team."

"The Sea Crest Church has birth and burial records for explorers, sailors, and architects who founded Sea Crest.

"Direct them to pick up a bookmark from the desk that says, 'I save your place in a book.'"

"The Sea Crest Cemetery also has its own Pirate's section. These are clues for this part of the scavenger hunt."

"Please find out the date that Black Beard died from his grave marker. Either take a picture or write it on a sheet of paper."

"We'll have some fake/toy pirate coins lying on top of Black Beard's tombstone. Pick up a coin from the top of a gravestone."

"Pick a daisy from the flower garden border of the cemetery."

Mary Beth asked, "How can we start a hunt so everyone is not going the same way at the same time?"

Antonio laughed, saying, "The easiest way is to mix up the order of items or clues so every group gets the same list in a different order."

Mary Beth laughed, "That should also give the players much more fun. They won't know they all have different orders on their lists? I love it!"

Antonio was troubled as he admitted, "You know, Mary Beth, I am concerned about one thing."

She was surprised, "What do you mean? I think everything we've got will produce a terrific scavenger hunt."

"Well, the one thing we need to figure out is that although it's a fund raiser for The Sea Crest Lighthouse, it's always nice to give something resembling a prize to the winner or winners. I'm not sure what we should do in this case. I expect everyone who enters the contest will thoroughly enjoy completing the game. Since no time limits are involved, everyone would qualify as a winner."

"I see what you mean. I may have a good answer. What do you think if everyone who completes the Scavenger Hunt receives an engraved brick for the walkway in front of the Sea Crest Museum with their name and date? In fact, I've heard of some lighthouses selling the bricks or steps of a lighthouse to raise funds."

"Mary Beth, that's brilliant! What if the team is a family affair?"

"I vote that every man, woman, and child earned their own brick. What a fantastic way to show that we're all working together to build a better community. As those children grow older, they'll remember that they are important and valuable to Sea Crest.

"Yes," said Mary Beth, "We need to inform them ahead of time that all the participants of this scavenger hunt will be awarded this meaningful engraved brick to create the walkway into the Sea Crest Museum."

"We should get this list of rules and rules printed as soon as possible. We need to be sure the clues have to be mixed up so they aren't all crowding into the same area at once."

Chapter Thirty

"Mary Beth, I have another idea I'd like to run by you," said Antonio with a mischievous smile.

"Well, ask away. So far, you're batting a hundred percent!"

"I'm a little thirsty, and I remember a half-marathon I was involved in once. It was a Trail Run track event. It was a blast to run, and after it was over, all the runners were invited to have free root beer floats as part of a participation reward."

"That sounds like an inspiring idea for our event!" exclaimed Mary Beth. "How can we use it?"

"Let's see. I overheard Maggie talking about her mom's pies that she plans to bake for the 'Best Pie Contest.' I think pie à la Mode is the tastiest way to enjoy it. I wonder if we could get a sponsor to supply the ice cream for the pie and root beer floats."

"Yes," chimed in Mary Beth. "We could also approach a root beer soda company to donate our other main ingredient. That would be a huge attraction and a nice way to hydrate people. How hard is it to make a root beer float?"

Antonio knew this one, "It's easy. The simplest ones have only those two ingredients. We must make sure they're smooth and creamy. To make the very best, they should be served in a tall glass, like a float glass. Do we have a kitchen supply house that would let us rent or donate our use of this kind of glassware? They appear very thick and probably survive without breakage or chipping."

Mary Beth said, "I'll see if the Sea Crest Restaurant could handle this, either with their private supply or with their many contacts. They are extremely supportive of all Sea Crest community endeavors."

Antonio added, "That's great. It's best if the glasses are extra frosty or chilled beforehand. What if we had a special setup with a cart and a freezer to achieve that?"

"That reminds me of the old-fashioned flower carts. I love it!"

As an afterthought, Antonio said," Of course, we'll also need both spoons or straws and lots of napkins for our public to enjoy them."

Mary Beth laughed, "Do you think whipped cream is a bit over the top?"

They happily contemplated how happy they felt at this moment in time.

Chapter Thirty-One

Mary Beth glanced at her watch and declared alarmingly, "Oh goodness, I'm late for my lunch date. I've got to run. Can I meet you tomorrow at the same time and continue with our planning?"

Antonio was also shocked at the time and late for his own appointment. He practically ran as he hurried away, "Wow, I had no idea it was this late. I've got to run! See you tomorrow!

A few minutes later, Mary Beth rushed into Maggie's house and stood looking out of breath and disheveled as she presented herself to Maggie, Kate, and Grace. "I'm so sorry I'm late! Time just got away from us, and I just remembered our Mah Jongg game."

Kate said, "That's fine. That gave us extra time to look at our new Mah Jongg cards with this year's winning tile combinations."

"Oh no," cried Mary Beth.

Maggie's Great Dane, Misha, was all prancing around, wondering why Mary Beth was so keyed up. She was usually calm and collected. What was wrong?

Mary Beth admitted, "I didn't even bring mine. I got my new card in the mail from the National Mah Jongg League this week. But I was rushing around trying to get ready to meet with Doctor Lewis about Antonio, and I never thought about it."

"That's okay," said Grace. "I ordered two cards as usual, just in case we needed it."

Maggie asked, "Did you have to look at the new winning hands for this year? I saw one with the winds and dragons that will be very hard to get, but it's worth 45 points instead of the normal 25 points."

Kate smiled as she threatened, "Oh, I'm going to try it often. By the way, what did you guys think of this year's math tile combinations?"

"I'm not sure how often I'll surprise you with using them, but I'll certainly try to keep you from using them," stated Grace as she handed her extra card to Mary Beth.

"Wow," murmured Mary Beth. "Look at what they came up with for this year's date hand. It's one of the hardest hands to put together and count for the most points because you can't use any jokers. However, if I'm not dealt any jokers to start the game, rest assured, that's what I'm trying for!"

Mary Beth was trying to distract them from the unusual late arrival, which was totally out of character. Maggie had seen her with Antonio earlier, and she wasn't going to let her get away with this. "Well," she said with a sparkle in her eyes. "We were just saying whatever you were doing must have been very important. After all, you called this meeting."

They almost burst out laughing at Mary Beth as they set up the tiles for Mah Jongg and passed the pieces of pizza around. This game was a perfect cover for their plans for 'Anonymous Acts of Kindness,' they always got into a game of Mah Jongg before they finished.

"Mary Beth was a little confused as she tried to explain. "Yes, I called this meeting to discuss some of our 'Anonymous

Acts of Kindness' today. Doctor Lewis invited Antonio and me for coffee and thought we should proceed with our plans for the Scavenger Hunt fund raiser. He said it would probably help Antonio's memory, so we agreed. We didn't realize how late it was getting."

Grace said innocently, with a hurt attitude, "Oh, I see. Did you find it more important to hang out with Antonio instead of us?"

"Of course not!"

"You weren't this upset while you were being kidnapped. Why is your face so red? Did he offend you in some way?"

"No! He's a perfect gentleman."

They all laughed, including Mary Beth, as she stated indignantly, "Just because you guys can't seem to conduct yourselves with any level of class doesn't mean that I can't behave like a perfect lady!"

"Well, we all stand corrected!" laughed Grace.

"Now, can we please talk about the case of my three new friends, Jack, Charlie, and Bill.

Maggie agreed, "Yes, surprisingly, these men are proving to be some of the best operatives we've got on this smuggling problem. They are all willing to help us and are the only ones with the knowledge to identify the smugglers running the illegal operation here at Sea Crest.

"Mary Beth was the first to notice that these men were not bad guys in this whole situation, but due to a case of mistaken identity, they thought she was also part of the smuggler's operation."

Mary Beth explained, "They clobbered Antonio because they thought he was part of the smuggler's ring that had threatened him at gun point. Jack thought Antonio was jumping their gold claim, and he hit him. Their intent was not to kill him but to keep him from taking their gold."

Maggie said, "Let's look at Jack's situation first. He is so far behind on these mortgage payments that it's been in foreclosure for the last couple of weeks. I checked at the bank this morning and put a 48-hour hold on the foreclosure until we could meet. Since he's in that position, he's got numerous other overdue bills and no end in sight.

"Next, Charlie, who has been out of work for a long time, is way behind on his bills. It literally breaks his heart that he can't even get Yoo-hoo for his little boy.

"Now, let's turn to Bill. His mom has a dire medical situation. They're behind in the bills and deeply in debt. She should see a specialist, but that's not happening due to the cost.

"These men have grown up together and trusted each other since they were kids. They heard the historical stories about the 'lost gold shipment' from the Civil War era and had some hunch on where it might be. They pooled what money they could scrape together and filed a claim for the gold rights on the land where the abandoned rail cars were exposed from the storm.

"The last time they were checking on it, hoping to be able to search for gold, the smugglers threatened them at gunpoint to stay away from the area, or they'd kill them.

"The next time they looked at the abandoned railroad tracks, they saw a guy nosing around and assumed he was one of the smugglers. They were unarmed but believed that Antonio was heavily armed. It was a case of mistaken identity. They didn't mean to kill anybody; they just wanted him to leave their gold claim alone. When they saw Mary Beth arrive and call 911, they assumed she was also one of the smugglers.

"They have happily agreed to help and work with us at the DEA on our smuggler problem. In fact, they worked last night, and we were delighted with their knowledge of the terrain in the area. They need jobs, and I always look for good people to work with us."

Mary Beth said, "As a Realtor, I'd be pleased to get them housing in our community, well within their means, if they take the jobs you offer. I don't know their present homes, but our area has some excellent homes. I'll work toward that end, given the chance."

Kate added, "I've spoken to others at the Coast Guard Medical Center, and we've got some of the finest medical professionals in the country. They will take Bill's mother as a patient at no charge under my advisement, and if there is a future financial problem, it will be passed on to me."

Grace said, "I can look up the historical records that are filed on the abandoned railroad section in which the railroad cars and tracks are exposed and clear any problems on their access. Their gold claim is precisely what it's there for. To keep others out until the claim is exhausted and cleared of precious metals."

Maggie closed with the promise "to make sure the mortgages are completely paid in full, so these guys can start with a clean slate. As always, the three men will not know how things got paid or who did it. Bill will be told of a study or a grant to care for his mom, and she'll receive no medical bills. She'll get the best care available."

"If they take Maggie up on her employment offer, the three men will receive hefty signing bonuses and a benefit package, which is out of this world."

The meeting was closed, and the Mah Jongg game began.

Chapter Thirty-Two

The following morning, Antonio thought He'd do some fact-checking on finding precious metals. Antonio thought he'd do some digging himself on gold claims and strikes, so he took to his computer.

"Let's see. It shows the BLM. What is that? Okay, it's one of nine bureaus under the Interior Department. The Bureau of Land Management's roots go back to America's founding.

"Here is some helpful information from the BLM about how to stake a claim. The person who found the loot may or may not get a reward: that decision is made by the Secretary of State 'in whatever way he thinks fit.'

He skipped down to the part about finding treasure or valuables on public land –

"It explains you would put it in your pocket. Then, you'd carefully note the GPS location, abandon the rest of your hiking plans, and carefully examine the surrounding area to look for a surface outcrop. If you found one, you would note the GPS location, run, not walk to the BLM office and file a claim.

He scrolled down to what pertained to gold.

"Gold nuggets are generally formed in water courses - streams and rivers - where the gold particles are tumbled and pushed together

until they meld. Gold from a lode is rarely free from the rock (usually quartz) it was deposited in. So, check carefully the place where you're walking. Is it gravel, like an ancient stream bed? Quickly go home, get a gold pan and a shovel, then start working back up the stream bed. Dig down to the bedrock every few yards and wash a few pans, looking for gold dust traces. You will almost certainly find some of the nuggets formed where you found them.

"Keep working upstream until the gold disappears. Then you know the outcrop is in the hillside, above and just behind you. Find it, chip out as much gold as you can carry, and then hurry to the BLM office to file a claim.

"Now, here's something pretty interesting. While you're at it, you may also file a placer claim on the area where you found the nugget. You never know.

"Let's see what this is down the page -

"Why does the government take part in any treasure discovered by a person?

"There are various potential reasons since different countries have different sets of laws. Remember that 'finders keepers' is part of a nursery rhyme, not a legal principle.

"However, sometimes, in the U.S., the adage 'finders keepers' is real.

"Example - In 2013, a California couple was out walking their dog and discovered 1,400 gold coins worth $10 million on their property. Since the discovery was made on their land, it was theirs to sell, which they absolutely had to do.

"In the U.S. - Anything contained in the land you own is yours, and anything on land you don't own is not yours, even if you find it. The government has no direct interest in it, though you are held liable for taxes based on the value of your find. Suppose you turned up a lost cache of Spanish gold coins on your ranch in Arizona. In that case, you'd have to pay hefty income tax, but the government would have no say in what happened to the coins themselves.

"He discovered some rules, although they aren't as gold digger-friendly. The term 'Coin' includes any metal token which was, or can reasonably be assumed to have been, used or intended for use as or instead of money.

'Precious metal' means gold or silver.

Antonio also made notes on objects that were found. He found this interesting but a little confusing.

When an object is found, it is part of the same find as another object if — (a) they are found together, (b) the other object was found earlier in the same place where they had been left together, (c) the other object was found earlier in a different place. Still, they had been left together and had become separated before being found.

(5) If the circumstances in which objects are found can reasonably be taken to indicate that they were together at some time before being found, the objects are to be presumed to have been left together unless shown not to have been.

Yikes! Antonio stopped doing his research at this time. He had a headache.

Chapter Thirty-Three

When Antonio and Mary Beth met to resume their Scavenger Hunt planning, they made their way up to the Sea Crest Church.

Mary Beth explained, "The town was named by Sir Michael Chambers, the captain of the Sea Crest schooner that sunk off the coast. Many of the details are recorded in his handwritten journal that will be in the Sea Crest Museum."

"Some of the things we found in his journal were letters about his upcoming journey to America. One of these letters revealed that he was instrumental in the women's suffrage and the anti-slavery movement. In fact, we saw correspondence from Eliza Wigham from Edinburgh, Scotland, and her sister Mary Edmundson from Ireland. They raised money to finance Sir Michael Chambers and his Sea Crest ship. His family were neighbors of Eliza Wigham, and his mother was a good friend of both these sisters."

"This explains a lot of how he was raised and his beliefs at the time of his voyage."

Antonio wanted to know, "Boy, that sounds extraordinary. Do you think the journal will be on display in the new museum?"

"I believe that's the plan. The journal is a personal window into Captain Michael Chamber's beliefs that molded his actions and ruled his life.

"Here are a couple of insights from his journal. He explains that most sailors did not know how to swim. His answer was to teach them how to swim with a portable snap-together waterproof swimming pool."

"First, everyone learns to float.
Then everyone must learn to swim!
There was no loss of life when the Sea Crest schooner
wrecked off the coast!
Everyone used their swimming skills to get ashore."

They eventually retrieved many of the goods on board, which helped them survive. They built the Sea Crest Lighthouse and founded the Town of Sea Crest."

"Our church has a wealth of historical information recorded in the church library. One of the articles was a copy of a picture of a pirate grave. The explanation of the engraving on the headstone suggests that this is the grave of one of Blackbeard's crew. The engraving says, 'The crew member repented his sins whilst being cared for in his twilight days, by the vicar of the church.' The article goes on to say, 'Most pirates were buried at sea, so this is a rare find.'"

"Grace recently found this story of the first female lightkeeper in Michigan. We believe it was written by a present-day ancestor who wrote about her great-grandmother. We're not sure, but it seems to have been written in the last decade."

Mary Beth opened the letter and relayed the story as follows:

Lost at Sea

March 31, 1849, Captain Peter Shook, the lightkeeper at the Pointe Aux Braques Lighthouse, drowned.

His boat capsized in a storm on Lake Huron, and he met a watery death. His body, as well as all three others on board, were never found.

As was the custom during that era, they often looked to a family member to replace an injured or deceased keeper. Sometimes, that job fell to the courageous wives and children of the lightkeeper. Recorded history shows numerous female lightkeepers in America who bravely held those jobs for short periods of up to half a century.

Those forgotten stories of life-saving survival at these dangerous and remote locations included mourning the loss of their loved one and caring for the surviving family members. The reality of these tragic events also meant that the job of managing the entire workload and responsibility of being a lighthouse keeper fell entirely on the shoulders of the family.

Peter Shook was survived by his wife Catherine and their eight children. In 1849, Catherine Shook was appointed the first female lighthouse keeper in the State of Michigan.

Sadly, in Catherine's case, we find the tragic death of her husband set in motion a relentless ripple effect that engulfed the entire lighthouse's function. However, this harsh reality was similarly repeated in the lives of all the lightkeeper's families who lost a loved one.

Shortly after Peter's death, a house fire broke out between the kitchen and the ceiling. She was severely burned in a courageous attempt to save the flames from spreading to the main house. As a result of the fire, her family lost their dwelling and most of their furniture and belongings. Through the following treacherous winter months, it's reported that they had little or no heat. Due to the capsized supply vessel, they had little of their usual allotment of food. The conditions were intolerable. The family was forced to stay in a small makeshift structure under terrible living conditions until the Lighthouse Superintendent was able to have their house rebuilt in 1850.

Due to poor health, Catherine Shook could not continue, and she resigned from her position in 1851. She moved to New Baltimore, Michigan, where she died nine years later.

Today, a Pointe Aux Barques Lighthouse visit will show the same strong, statuesque, white tower. Their museum also offers many historical artifacts and antiques that graced the property over a hundred years ago.

It shows another unique glimpse into Michigan's lighthouse history. Around 1876, the Michigan Lighthouse Conservatory began distributing its now-famous Portable Traveling Libraries to its lightkeepers. These rugged wooden boxes held an assortment of 40-50 of the best books of their time.

Inside the top of each box was attached a list of its inventory. A Bible was often included, but the rest was a variety of reading material suitable for the family, a toy doll, and simple games. These treasured libraries would be exchanged with other lighthouses quarterly. Out-of-date or damaged books were replaced as needed. The grateful keepers and their families had an excellent opportunity that even the public lacked. Unbelievable as it seems, during the 1800s, there were more lighthouses than public libraries. Granted, you would have beautiful libraries in your mansions if you were from wealthy families such as the Rockefellers, the Mellon Family, or the Du Pont Family. However, ordinary citizens did not have access to this volume of books. The Pointe Aux Barques Lighthouse has an excellent replica of one of these weathered Portable Traveling Library boxes on display.

I spent several days at the cabins of The Pointe Aux Barques Lighthouse in Port Huron, Michigan. I learned of the lighthouse's history, the museum, and the life-saving station being built on the property.

I was pleasantly surprised to learn that they have several lighthouse celebrations and events during the summer, including beauti-

ful weddings at the top of the lighthouse. That is a dream come true for most lighthouse lovers.

I have always found lighthouses from around the world irresistible. I'm especially drawn to their history and find it incredible to learn about each lighthouse I visit. I marvel at the courageous lives of lightkeepers, and I'm fascinated by their heroic spirit.

Many people today view the rich history of lighthouses through a lens of romance and adventure. Our imaginations display the splendor we see from the top of these tall, beautiful towers. The lightkeepers were truly brave, superhuman people, and their lives are worth remembering.

Mary Beth and Antonio solemnly looked at each other in shared silence.

Antonio felt the soft scent of Chanel, ever so faintly, touch his memory. *What does this mean? Why do I feel like this? I want to take Mary Beth's hand in mine. Why? Who is she to me? Why does she feel familiar to me?*

Mary Beth was responding to the story's last words: *"Courageous, superhuman people whose lives are worth remembering. The only similar feeling I have about a superhuman was a week ago when I was dancing with Zorro. Yes, I'll remember that for the rest of my life."*

Just then, a robust, jolly chaplain came bounding into the church library! "Sorry, I didn't mean to interrupt... Why hello, Mary Beth, I think it is?"

Mary Beth was shocked as well, "Hello, Chaplain O'Reilly. I didn't know you were visiting here."

Chaplain O'Reilly was shocked to see Philip standing beside her. As he held out his hand, Mary Beth promptly stepped in and said, "This is Antonio. He's working with Special Agent Maggie Jensen. Still, he's been dealing with temporary amnesia for the past few days. He's under the care of Doctor Lewis at the Coast Guard Medical Center."

The chaplain was taken aback but cordially shook Philip's hand. "So happy to meet you... Antonio. I know Doctor Lewis very well. He's a good doctor. Let me know if I can help in any way. I'll be visiting through the Scavenger Hunt Fund Raiser."

Antonio finally spoke as a tiny crack in his thoughts felt the chaplain's warmth. "Hello, happy to meet you. Mary Beth and I are working together on the Scavenger Hunt."

Chapter Thirty-Four

Just about that time, Jack was getting ready to join Charlie and Bill to drive over to Sea Crest to prepare for his new assignment at the FBI Special Drug Smuggling Enforcement Detail when the doorbell rang.

He took a quick look out the window, and his heart sank. *"Oh no! I recognize the man from the bank. He's coming to foreclose on our house."*

He called to his wife, "Honey, I guess we ran out of time. That man from the bank is here."

"Oh no!" she gasped tearfully as they opened the front door.

The man looked up as he walked into the room. With a perplexed look, he was busy shuffling numerous papers in his hand. He finally muttered, "Well, I'm not sure what happened here, but there will not be a foreclosure on your house."

"What do you mean?"

"I don't know what is happening, but it appears your house has been paid in full. You no longer have a mortgage. You own it free and clear."

"You've got to be kidding! I don't understand what you're talking about!" pleaded Jack as his wife burst into tears.

"It was on my desk when I came in this morning," the man said. "It's all sealed and private, but the judge stated that the funds had been paid, which is true. But the case is sealed, so the bank doesn't know how it got paid. However, it's paid in full!"

Jack and his sobbing wife were speechless.

"Anyway," the man continued. "Here's the title to your home. No hard feelings now, okay? Sorry, we had to be so hard on you guys. Bye."

Jack and his wife were both crying tears of joy now!

Across town, Charlie's doorbell rang around the same time. Charlie was finishing breakfast with his wife and son. His son ran to the door with him to see a man from the same bank with the same confused look on his face.

The man reported that all his outstanding bills had been paid in full. All his 'past-due' bills in his drawer were now paid, including the outstanding balance due. He didn't know who or how it happened, but the case was sealed and closed.

Following the exit of that perplexed gentleman, another truck showed up at the house. The driver delivered a brand-new refrigerator and several cases of Yoo-hoo Chocolate Drink.

The final visitor went to Bill's house. He told Bill that some anonymous entity had paid the total debt of his mom's medical bills in full. As the official courier said goodbye, he added another odd thing, "The whole case was sealed, so I have no idea how that was even accomplished. It also looks like many other outstanding bills have been erased, but the medical bills alone were huge."

The man shook his head as he opened his car door to leave and uttered, "I don't understand it!"

Bill and his mom were still reeling from the shock of this news when a second visitor arrived. She was from the Coast

Guard Medical Center. When Bill answered the door, Kate introduced herself. "Hello. I'm Coast Guard Search and Rescue helicopter pilot Kate Jensen. I wonder if I could talk with your mom briefly."

Bill's mom was seated at the table, and Kate went in and sat down to talk with her. Kate introduced herself and asked how she was feeling today.

Kate took her vitals and had a heartfelt talk with her. Kate explained that his mom qualified for a special grant that never has to be paid back. This grant offers medical assistance to patients matching their exact medical needs. They can supply the specialists and experts she needs.

Kate offered to get the very best care to get Bill's mom feeling well soon, with no strings attached.

As Kate said goodbye, Bill and his mom were filled with genuine hope and gratitude.

Later that day, when the three men arrived at the DEA/FBI headquarters, they were offered new employment with an excellent benefits package and sizable signing bonuses. All three men happily accepted their new jobs with the Drug Prevention Division, beginning immediately.

Their afternoon meeting was scheduled with Mary Beth, their previous kidnapping victim. She was delighted they had great jobs and some additional news for them.

She had several home listings in the area if they wanted to relocate to the Town of Sea Crest. The men reviewed the printouts and set up appointments to check them out over the next few days.

Chapter Thirty-Five

That evening, Maggie followed through with Project Red Blood. That was a special surveillance-driven operation in which the FBI Drug Enforcement Agency carried out their well-practiced, two-night sting operation. It combined both local and federal law enforcement teams. Since Antonio was not available to participate yet, his team was still heavily involved.

In fact, they were in charge of particular Black Hawk aircraft to surveil the vessels in the area after dark with their night vision apparatus. These specialized avionics support electronic systems and equipment designed explicitly for Drug Enforcement nationally and worldwide.

Meanwhile, the real smugglers were discussing their dilemma. "That 'drug drop' better come off without any interference."

"It's lucky we had our drugs packaged in waterproof bags earlier. We could drag them behind the boat unnoticed. Their weight prevented them from floating to the surface. We better check out the drop zone early and ensure he doesn't break the perimeter. We need that money!"

"If we blow this deal, that's the end for us."

Maggie planned, *"Tonight, we should be able to see any boats of interest with their lights turned off. The helicopter can spot a vessel in the water up to 10 miles away. Air and Marine Operations will be able to detect any criminal activity this evening.*

"The water will be rough with seven-foot waves. Any vessel with its lights turned out will probably be conducting illegal activity.

"The Black Hawk helicopters can guide the Coast Guard and Special Drug Forces to their locations. Their radar will take them right to it."

As the night became exceedingly more turbulent, the airmen in the helicopters targeted their night-vision equipment to show two vessels, ten miles ahead, with their lights out, trying to get to the shore. It looked like one might have been scouting for the safety of the other.

They radioed the coordinates to the Coast Guard vessels, who raced to navigate alongside the boats. One of the boats steered right up even with the beach and then rammed it on the tree-lined banks. Three men jumped out and abandoned their boat, running into the thick, overgrown mangrove roots and trees, making it almost impossible to escape.

The Coast Guard apprehended the drug runners and took them aboard the USCG Cutter in handcuffs. The second vessel of smugglers was so close behind that it couldn't avoid crashing into the sandy banks. They were also captured and arrested. Both boats were seized, and their contraband was towed back to the Coast Guard base.

This overnight raid on the smugglers was a triple score for the DEA.

The drugs had been split up before they left Columbia. That meant they would only lose half their drugs and profit if they were discovered. In this sting operation, they had 2,000 kilos of crystal meth, and drugs, in 59 total packages.

The other big hit was a box full of contraband. There was a box wrapped in waterproof bubble wrap. When the agents opened it, it was full of little picture frames. They didn't look right when they held them up to the light! One of the airmen asked, "They must be taking over $10,000 into the country."

Maggie wore her white gloves and held the bill up to the light. *"The watermark is a characteristic security feature of authentic banknotes. Many new bills use a watermark that is actually a replica of the face on the bill. On other banknotes, it is just an oval spot."*

She looked closely at it and finally said, "These are all 100.00 dollar counterfeit bills."

They each pulled on their gloves and started counting the bills, one at a time. By the time they were finished, they had counted $104,000.

Antonio was just an observer toward the end of the operation; however, he looked long and hard at the boat coming ashore about a mile away. He took the best binoculars that were available and zeroed in on it. "Yes, they're hauling several white bags that look suspiciously covered in seaweed."

The Coast Guard crew jumped immediately to the race against time to catch them before they landed and unloaded.

Antonio explained, "They might also try to escape by water; however, the smugglers didn't have a GoBoat, so we'll catch them quickly."

After a short time, the crew master shouted, "Nice call, Antonio. We've got them!"

Maggie congratulated the efforts of everyone involved. "All in all, it was a super successful sting operation for all who participated. I'm proud of each and everyone who made this happen. You worked seamlessly together as a team. Thank you!"

Chapter Thirty-Six

The following morning, the BLM - Bureau of Land Management representative met with Jack, Charlie, Bill, and both Maggie and Mary Beth to discuss the 'lost gold' claim status that they filed.

Maggie began, "I've looked into how 'lost treasure' claims are handled in our county. That includes the Town of Sea Crest and the surrounding seashore community. We want to ensure their claim is reserved if they move into the Sea Crest area. In fact, our towns are situated right next to each other. The boundary line runs through the cliffs and divides the sand dunes, splitting the area almost in two as it runs down to the water. The abandoned railroad tracks and train cars are scattered throughout the combined area.

"They had a copy of BLM's brochure covering the casual-use activities in hand to refer to. Casual use is those that cause only negligible disturbance of public lands and resources.

"For example, activities not involving earthmoving equipment or explosives may be considered casual use. For most casual-use activities, there is no requirement to notify the BLM. However, State Directors may establish specific areas where the cumulative effects of casual use have resulted in, or are expected to result in, more than negligible disturbance. The BLM must be contacted 15 calendar days before beginning activities to determine whether the individual or group must submit a notice or plan of operations (43 CFR 3809.31(a)). Contact the local BLM office for the boundaries of these State Director-designated areas."

"What about treasure hunters and the like?" asked Jack.

Maggie continued, "I was told there are lost treasures scattered worldwide, long ago hidden. These include lost mines and buried precious gold, silver, and copper stashes. The numerous sunken ships hold vast amounts of hidden wealth. Treasure hunters spend countless hours researching and relocating buried treasures worth millions!"

Jack agreed, "We wanted to secure a claim on that area. We were told we needed to ensure that no one had a current claim on the property with the newly exposed tracks. We paid for them to run a search for us, filled out the paperwork, and paid for the charge for the claim."

"Well," agreed the BLM representative. "Everything looks in order. Moving into this area does not affect your claim, so you can now work your gold claim."

Chapter Thirty-Seven

Mary Beth and Antonio were to meet around noon at the Sea Crest Church and continue to wander around the Sea Crest Cemetery to finish up the Scavenger Hunt layout and clues.

Mary Beth found herself changing her clothes several times for some inexplicable reason. She looked at herself in the floor-length mirror one more time; "At last, this looks perfect!" She looked like she had just stepped out of an advertisement for a casual beach sundress in a high-end magazine.

"Now I'll pick one of my long-bob, red hair wigs and be ready." As she flew out the door, it never occurred to her that Antonio wouldn't even recognize her.

Antonio was sitting on a bench outside the church when a car drove up and parked in the lot. He watched out of the corner of his sunglasses as a knock-out dream of a lady in a crisp navy and white sundress got out and waved to him.

He thought, *"She can't mean me."* He looked around and found no one else in the area. *"So, I guess I'll wave back."* He waved very self-consciously.

"Oh yeah, I forgot, I've got amnesia. I might know her." He waved again like he knew her. *"Nothing ventured, nothing gained!*

"Wow, now she's coming right over to me. Maybe she needs directions."

Mary Beth said, "Wow, Antonio. We've got a beautiful day to investigate the cemetery, don't we?"

Antonio practically jumped out of his skin as he yelled, "Mary Beth? Is that you?"

She just laughed as she sat down beside him and said, "Of course, silly, who did you think I was?"

Antonio turned and looked her full in the face and realized how beautiful she looked. "Well, what did you do to your hair?"

She smiled and explained. "I didn't even remember, but I put this wig on because it would be windy up here. Don't you like it?"

"Yes, you're a knockout in it. I don't remember much about someone wearing a wig, but I might have seen you in it before. I'm sure I thought you looked nice then, too."

That finally got her attention. She whispered, "Antonio, I'm sorry I startled you. I have lots of wigs of all types. Everyone knows I have ones for all my dance costumes, and I change them out often as the mood suits me."

Antonio thought of that for a moment, then without thinking twice, he blurted out, "Could you do me a big favor?"

She turned and looked him in the eyes and quietly said, "Of course, anything."

"Well, please don't change your perfume. It's wonderful, and it makes me feel better. I think it means something important to me."

"Well, that's the last thing I thought he was going to say!"

She replied, "Of course, that's easy. Chanel is the only scent I wear."

Chapter Thirty-Eight

As they entered the Sea Crest Cemetery, Antonio asked, "How much do you know about Pirates?"

Walking through the cemetery was like a look backward in time.

She answered, "I know this whole Sea Crest area was historically prime pirate territory. Full of Swashbucklers and Buccaneers. In fact, we have the remains of the famous Black Beard pirate buried here in the Pirates Section of this cemetery."

"Yes, I read about him this morning. It sounds real, but I understand that famous pirates are often buried in multiple graveyards up and down the coast from North to South America, plus the whole Caribbean. I'll have to rely on your expertise; however, if it's famous folklore, we must include it in the scavenger hunt. Our public will relish the idea of him being buried in our cemetery."

"I agree. Our public demands it!" she laughed. "You know, I never even thought about how much fun it is to plan this event. You are an unexpected pleasure to be around."

"Oh, you mean when you're scaring me to death? You, with your disguises and talk of pirates. You seem to be well-versed in the occult, my dear." He immediately waved his finger at her and followed up laughing with, "And don't let that slip of the tongue fool you. You're a case, and you know it. I'm an innocent man scrambling to find his memory while you flit around in that get-up, outrageous sun dress and wig."

"You're going to get it!" She cried, laughing, "Take that back right now!"

Just then, the jolly Chaplain O'Reilly came bounding out of the side door of the church. "Hey, did you guys hear anyone screaming out here? Oh, Mary Beth. Hello, Dear."

"Hello, Chaplain. We were just fooling around out here. Antonio was teasing me because he didn't recognize me in my wig. Among other things," she couldn't hide a fit of giggling again as she cried, "He said I was trying to scare him to death."

Her innocent pretense of complete helplessness caused all three of them to laugh.

The Chaplain paused as he announced, "Boy, Mary Beth, I never saw this side of you in Tahiti last month."

The laughter stopped!

Antonio felt a tiny wave of recognition move over him as he thought, *"Why does that make me feel so odd? It's like a secret, hiding in plain sight. They share something about Tahiti."*

Antonio cautiously asked, "Mary Beth? You were in Tahiti?"

She said, "Yes, one of my friends was there for a short project, and I thought it would be fun to go over for a few days also."

The Chaplain didn't know if this line of talk would be good or bad for Antonio, aka Philip, so he jumped in with laughter and a warning, "Okay, enough of this horseplay. We should be ashamed of partying in the cemetery, of all places!"

He chuckled as he left, thinking, *"They will be perfect for each other."*

Antonio and Mary Beth sheepishly looked at each other and tried to stop the flow of enjoyment that they seemed to bring out in each other.

Antonio broke the silence with a glint in his eyes, as he remarked, "Well, I, for one, am utterly shocked at your lack of decorum!"

Mary Beth quickly defended herself, "Hey! I'm usually a picture of etiquette and dignity," she bragged with a chuckle and a toss of her head. "I'm famous for my demureness and restraint. I'm sure I'm overcompensating for your lack of manners, and I hope you learn what good behavior looks like. Then you can adjust your own 'decorum' when you regain your memory."

"Wow, great zinger," he laughed!

Antonio whispered as he disclosed, "I'm sure this is the most fun I've ever had strolling around a cemetery."

"I think it's just the hope of having some refinement and culture rub off from hanging around with me. You have something special to look forward to."

"Then what's your excuse? You seem delighted to spend time with a sophisticated, handsome, gracious man you continue to scare and play tricks on!"

After a solid five minutes of trying to come to a reasonable explanation of why they found themselves in this crazy situation, they continued to smile as they roamed around the cemetery.

Antonio asked, "What are some of the best grave markers we should highlight or draw attention to from a historical viewpoint?"

"Well, let's see," she said thoughtfully. "I'd love to be able to find the grave of one of the female lightkeepers."

Antonio looked surprised. "I thought women were considered 'bad luck' by many sailors. If a woman stepped aboard, it was perilous."

"Reign of Terror was spoken of by the pirates, mutineers, and other rogue seafarers. In fact, folklore has tales of women who walked the plank. However, there is not much evidence that it actually happened," she replied.

"I've heard that Jack Sparrow in the movie, 'Pirates of the Caribbean,' had a girlfriend, and he was always trying to get her on board," said Antonio.

"That is only fictional for the book and movies. I don't know if it's real. However, I do know of a few female lightkeepers who were unbelievably brave and saved many lives. I'd love to find a grave of somebody like that for our scavenger hunt!"

"Would they be buried in the pirate's cemetery?"

"I don't think so, simply because I'd assume their family and extended family would be buried in more of a family plot area. This wouldn't be the case for famous pirates.

"While we look for a female lightkeeper, I could tell you about one of my favorites. By the way, my friend Grace is also the Sea Crest town historian. She discovered some correspondence from Abbie Burgess, the lightkeeper in Maine, to the Sea Crest lightkeeper's family."

"Wow, that's interesting," he said. "I'd love to hear about it."

"Great. The first letter describes moving to the lighthouse with her family when she was fourteen. Some of the lighthouses are built on the mainland, and some have a small walkway or bridge-type access. However, their lighthouse was located twenty miles distance out in the ocean.

"It was a rough location with fierce, stormy weather, especially in difficult winters. The light station included two wooden towers attached to both ends of the keeper's dwelling."

Antonio asked, "That's unusual. Two separate lights?"

"Yes, and the keeper had to light a total of 28 Argand lamps with whale oil and keep them burning and the wicks trimmed from sunset until sunrise every night."

"Wow! What a job!" said Antonio. "Don't tell me that girl would help do all that."

"Yes, she did all that and more. Her mother was an invalid and unable to climb the stairs or help with the lights in either of the towers. Abbie did much of the work, helped with the lights, and cared for the house so her father could fish for lobsters and sail to Rockland to sell them. This was probably not appreciated by the lighthouse board, as additional income to government pay was frowned upon in those days. But the worst was yet to come."

"Oh no," said Antonio. "That sounds serious. What happened?"

"Their shipment of supplies, due twice a year from the mainland, had not arrived, and their food and oil for the lamps were running dangerously low. One beautiful day with a clear blue sky, Abbie watched her father leave in their boat to the mainland for supplies and medicine for her mother. A northeastern storm roared in and washed over the island within the hour. Her father was unable to return for four weeks."

"That's terrible!"

"Abbie saw the water rushing into the ground floor of the keeper's cottage. Since they had chickens outside, she rushed out, corralled 5, swooped them up, and ran into the tower with them. One got away and was swept away immediately.

"As the tide came in, the sea rose so fast and furious that they looked for some way to save their lives. She looked to the towers as their only hope.

"First, she rescued her mother, then her two young sisters, and managed to help them up the stairs into one of the towers. She desperately grabbed what supplies she could salvage.

"A moment later, they watched while their keeper's cottage was completely demolished and swept away before their eyes."

"That's unbelievable!" Antonio whispered in awe.

"She described the next four terrifying weeks as such violent weather that no one could return to help them. During this harrowing time, they barely had enough food and warmth. She recalls that she was extremely exhausted by her labors, but she could keep the lights burning. 'Under God, I was able to perform all my accustomed duties as well as my father's.'"

Antonio said, "That's incredible!"

They sat down on a small bench in the cemetery. They didn't even realize that he had taken Mary Beth's hand.

Antonio asked, "Do you think we can find anything in the church records about who is buried here and where their tombstones are located?"

"It's worth a try. Maybe if we find it in the approximate dates and maritime categories for light keeper families," answered Mary Beth. "Maybe Grace can help us too. She also can access the information that covers the State of Maine."

She thought for a minute and then said, "While we're here, we should go ahead and check for information on the female lightkeepers and where they are buried."

As they headed back toward the church, Antonio said, "This is so exciting. It's like we're on our own Scavenger Hunt. Trying to solve a puzzle and adding important clues about who the brave, heroic female lightkeepers were."

"Yes," she replied. "I feel sad that you've lost your memory. Here I am, trying to remember what I was like as a young girl, and you probably can't retrieve a whole host of memories. I'm so sorry."

"Well, we can still admire the courage and strength of that amazing girl. She should have received a medal, but instead, I'm sure her quick thinking action was something which she demonstrated numerous times in her young life."

"Let's call Grace and see if she has any information or if she can meet with us," said Mary Beth as she placed the call."

A moment later, she asked Grace to meet them at the cemetery with anything to help them identify female lightkeepers buried there. Grace was excited as she volunteered, "Yes, I think I know the keeper you were talking about. I believe her letter was to one of our own female lightkeepers. I'll be right there!"

They stopped at a small bench in the cemetery, and as they sat, Antonio naturally draped his arm near her shoulders along the back of the bench. They didn't even realize how close they had become as they shared the thrill of discovering this amazing historical heroine. "We really need to add this story to our scavenger hunt no matter what else we learn," said Antonio.

"Yes, we'll have to include a clue about a female lightkeeper buried here. They'll have to locate her gravestone and take a picture or answer a question from the engraving if it's legible."

"Oh, here comes Grace," said Mary Beth. "She almost turned away, like she didn't recognize us."

Antonio quickly laughed as he pointed out, "She probably doesn't recognize your disguise. I'm not saying you look scary, but you'd be great in the FBI undercover."

Chapter Thirty-Nine

As Grace approached the couple, she stopped abruptly. *"I can't believe Antonio has his arm around Mary Beth. What's happened to them? Did Antonio regain his memory?".*

"Hello, how's it going?" she asked as she tried to cover her shock with pleasantries.

"Oh, just fine. Can you believe we might have a female lightkeeper right here in the Sea Crest Cemetery?" gushed Mary Beth.

"It's just one of several things that are hard to believe," stated Grace, as she wondered, *"What in the world is the state of your relationship? You look like a real couple!"*

As Antonio recapped the story that Mary Beth had described to him, he withdrew his arm from the back of the bench. He leaned forward so naturally that he didn't realize it had almost been practically around her shoulders. He finished by saying, "I know I'm still trying to recover my memory; however, I'm blown away by the heart and strength of this wonderful girl. We'd like to know how to honor the constant acts of sheer willpower and quick decision-making for the female lightkeepers who went above and beyond every day to save lives."

"The writer of the letter you mentioned was from a lighthouse up north in Maine," answered Grace. "Her name was Abbie, and she corresponded with the Sea Crest Lighthouse keepers for many years. However, that's not the end of her story. I'll have to find the letter, but if I remember correctly – she fulfilled these duties throughout her teen years and beyond.

"In fact, when her father retired, he persuaded one of his friends, Captain John Grant, to take his place as the next keeper. Abbie stayed on to train Grant on the lightkeeper job. A romance quickly blossomed between Abbie and Isaac Grant, the new keeper's son.

"A year later, they married, and she was officially appointed assistant keeper. They had several children while located there. Later, Isaac Grant was appointed to another Maine lighthouse, where Abbie was again the lightkeeper's assistant.

"She was an 'Assistant Keeper' for decades, although she trained the official light keepers at both of those lighthouses."

Grace smiled and declared, "The lady she was writing to was a keeper at the Sea Crest Lighthouse. Her name was Mrs. Elizabeth Chambers. She married Sir Michael Chambers and took over the keeper's duties after his death for five years. Then, it was passed on to their oldest son, Michael Chambers Jr.

Mary Beth expounded proudly, "Wow, she was the first woman lightkeeper in Sea Crest, and she was married to the builder and founder of the Town of Sea Crest and the Sea Crest Lighthouse.

"Yes," explained Grace. "That means she's Lady Chambers, buried next to Sir Michael Chambers in our Sea Crest Cemetery. The wife of a knight who is Knighted as Sir is known as 'Lady,' followed by her husband's surname, Lady Chambers."

"I'm doubly thrilled that you are such a wealth of information about our lighthouse and town," said Mary Beth.

"Well, I don't know everything," Grace admitted. "I've run across a few bits of gossip that say that a matchmaker was involved in finding a true love for Sir Michael Chambers."

"You're kidding!" gasped Mary Beth. "Was that even a real thing back then?"

"Is that even a real thing nowadays?" asked Antonio.

"Yes," piped up Grace. "Joe and I contacted one of them last year to see if they existed. We wanted to see if we could get any ideas for getting Maggie and James together. Of course, we weren't planning to get serious ourselves, but... this is a strange coincidence, isn't it?"

Grace slowly stopped talking and stared at Antonio and Mary Beth. After a pause, she muttered, "Do you think they thought we were meant to fall deeply in love, and they put a spell on us?"

"Well, where did you find a matchmaker anyway?" asked Mary Beth. "As for Maggie and James, they seemed to hate each other. Why did you want to match them up?"

Grace pointed out, "It was plain as day to us how they couldn't help but react to each other. I was either 'Love' or 'Hate,' and the reason for the hate disappeared when Kate and Michael were found unharmed and in love.

"Joe and I wanted to be sure they didn't miss their chance to fall in love. We thought a matchmaker would have an answer to solve that," Grace concluded.

Mary Beth looked at her watch and exclaimed, "Hey, I've got to run. I'm due at a meeting with Maggie."

"Yes," agreed Antonio. "Time sure flies when I'm planning this Scavenger Hunt. I'll see you later."

Grace couldn't wait to tell Joe, as she called him. "Hi, Joe. Guess who I just saw, and I think they are falling hard for each other?"

Chapter Forty

At about that same time, a young lady unloaded her suitcases at the Sea Crest Inn and headed inside. As she approached the main desk, a gentleman stepped out of a nearby elevator and collided head-on. He awkwardly grabbed her and carried them both down to the floor.

"Oh no! Are you okay?" cried Attorney Jeffrey Williams as he tried to get up and unsuccessfully help her simultaneously.

"Do I look okay?" she answered with a look of disdain as she jerked her arm away.

"Here, let me help," Jeffrey said as he knelt down and scooped up her laptop computer. Numerous papers were scattered within a five-foot wide area along with pens and a notebook, opened to 'Match-Maker' or 'Trouble-Maker'?

"Hey, what is all this about," asked Jeffrey as he looked at her suspiciously.

"It's none of your business," she responded with a superior attitude. "I'm sure you wouldn't understand, and furthermore, leave my stuff alone! You've done enough damage."

Jeffrey had never been spoken to with that attitude and couldn't believe she had the nerve to address him that way. As he looked her in the eye, he warned her quietly, "You are very rude. I don't know what you're up to but don't try anything in this town. We don't like match-makers or trouble-makers." With that, he placed her laptop on the floor and tossed, floated, and scattered her papers and 'stuff' around the entire area.

"Stop! What are you doing!" she cried as she tried to gather everything.

"Just proving that I haven't 'done enough damage' after all. And don't ever talk to anyone from Sea Crest with such a lack of respect. It just makes you look bad!"

Jeffery walked away with a confused feeling of satisfaction and yet regret. *"Who is she? I didn't mean to run smack dab into her. I was reading the Scavenger Hunt events for the next few days. I stepped out of the elevator, and she fell all over me on her way down to the floor."*

He also stopped in his tracks as he thought. *"Hey, where's the list of events I was reading? Don't tell me they're strewn all over the floor mixed up in her papers."*

He checked his pockets and hoped for a miracle. *"Wow! I was planning what to bid on. I always stay at the Sea Crest Inn and eat at the Sea Crest Restaurant. Now that crazy lady has my stuff!"*

He chuckled to himself. *"I really gave her a zinger at the end! 'It just makes You look bad.' Well, not that she could possibly look anything but good. However, she sure made me mad with her arrogant attitude."*

"I wonder who she is. Many people will visit the Scavenger Hunt Fund Raiser for the Museum."

He frowned. *"Maybe she's here with her boyfriend. He better have thick skin to put up with that mouth. Or maybe she's married."*

He finished with a deep sigh. *"Oh well, I'll never see her again, so who cares."* However, he took one last look over his shoulder, just in case he could see her again.

"Yes," he smiled in spite of himself. *"There she is, picking up all the junk she has. Wow, she's much prettier when she's not talking. Her appalling attitude doesn't match her looks."*

He decided to hang around longer and see what she did. *"Not exactly stalking, mind you. Just be in the vicinity for a couple of minutes. Well, I'm not loitering either. Just lingering. There, that sounds a lot better."*

Jeffery saw her finish picking up all her paraphernalia and thought, *"Okay, she's on the move."*

She dragged her suitcase behind her as she clutched her laptop and rearranged what felt like a ton of 'Stuff' in her arms. She made her way across the atrium to the check-in counter of the Sea Crest Inn.

"Hello, how may I help you?" asked the desk clerk with a smile.

Jeffery moseyed around to within earshot and pretended to read a paper.

The woman answered, "I have a reservation for one week."

"Great, may I have your name?

"Abigail Chambers."

The clerk paused and looked at the woman across from her. "Our town and lighthouse were founded by Sir Michael Chambers. Any relation?" she joked.

"That's what I'm here to find out," Abigail whispered with an emotional lump in her throat.

Chapter Forty-One

"What do you mean, Chaplain O'Reilly caught you laughing in the cemetery?" asked Maggie.

"Well, you had to be there," said Mary Beth. "But it sounded funnier when it was happening. At any rate, I think the details of Scavenger Hunt are ready to be set up, and the entry flyers printed with the secret clues."

"Wow, that was fast!"

"Yeah, I'm almost sad it's ending."

"Well, it's not really the end. We still have to set up the dance contest at the end."

"What are you talking about? What dance contest?"

"You were so busy that I didn't want to bother you with details, but we're going to have a silent auction, a town BBQ, and a seafood potluck supper, plus a dance contest to keep the money rolling in and make a final tally at the end of the night. The matching fund companies and organizations will want to know the outcome, plus the free advertising for their help."

Mary Beth was excited to hear this as she was planning one of the most significant events this town has ever seen. *"I've got a secret idea of my own for the dance part of the evening, and it is going to be a shocking, wonderful surprise if we can pull it off."*

Maggie finished her original plans and said, "I'll talk with you later about the details. By the way, good job with Antonio's memory problem. I'm sure you made all the difference to whatever happens with his memory. Thanks!"

Chapter Forty-Two

Early the following day, Mary Beth met with the Sea Crest Dance Studio students, ready for the rehearsal of their lives. "Thank you all for coming. It's been a long-time wish for most of us to do a flash mob event. We now have a golden opportunity to dance to some of our favorite musical numbers. Today, I will review the steps and music for our surprise flash mob at the Sea Crest Museum Fundraiser's picnic BBQ."

Everyone clapped their hands in excitement and gave each other high-fives as they started commenting and asking numerous questions, including, "Oh, I love this!" "Can you believe it? We're going to do a flash mob!" "What kind of music are we going to dance to?" "Are we going to sing too?" "How exciting!"

Mary Beth was beaming as she explained, "The dance routines are going to be ones we have all learned and practiced over the years here at the studio. We will use our familiar steps to flow and energize our moves to some of the best-known and loved songs from three dance styles.

"Have everyone from the past wedding celebrations do the traditional dance on the lighted snap-together dance floor. It can be placed right over the top of the sand. Since we're featuring the surprise flash mobs, we should make sure we have an extra-large dance floor."

One of the dancers asked, "What about our out-of-town family and friends? Can they practice the order of our routines and join us?"

"Absolutely," Mary Beth cried. "We want everyone to be involved, either singing along or joining us to dance. If you have friends who'd like to be part of this, ask them to practice the steps with you ahead of time so it will be easier to mix in, but tell them this is a 'surprise flash dance.' We are all sworn to secrecy! It won't have a brilliant impact on everyone unless we surprise them. That's half the fun!

"Okay, this might be the highlight of your dance endeavors, and I'll bet it will be the most fun! Our performance will start as the Sea Crest's BBQ and outstanding pot-luck picnic is well underway. First, they will dive into the best food in the county and the chili cook-off and pie-eating contest. Next, the judges will declare the winning contenders and hand out the blue ribbons.

"But just when they finish their meals and relax, we'll shake things up!"

"We'll have assistance from Jimmy, the disc jockey from the Masquerade Ball. He has agreed to help us with the music and produce one of the greatest flash mobs in history! He will be playing soundtracks of selections directly from the CD recordings. These selections will be instantly recognizable, and our goal is to have everyone singing along, dancing in the aisles, smiling, and clapping with joy!

"We'd like to start the surprise when he gets up from the BBQ and throws the cover off the sound equipment."

One of her friends said, "Suppose the picnickers recognize him from the Masquerade Ball at the Lighthouse?"

Mary Beth laughed, "In that case, they'll assume he will make some announcements. Maybe thank everyone for coming out to support the new museum. Possibly, they'll believe he's ready to tell who the Scavenger Hunt winners are or even say that it's the last call for bids on the silent auction items. They have ten minutes to finish and submit their highest bids.

"Jimmy will, in fact, signal all of us dancers that the flash mob will start momentarily. We must be ready to leave our seats and finish our conversations without giving away our surprise at what's coming next. The first selection will be from the Musical 'Mamma Mia,' featuring hits from 1970s supergroup ABBA."

"Wow," the dancers were thrilled at the chance to perform one of their favorite routines to ABBA's music. They danced around and gave each other 'high fives' as they shouted their approval. "We love that music!" "Which songs can we do?" "That's GREAT!"

Mary Beth explained, "The first few notes he plays will be stunning, loud, and beautiful as Jimmy starts with the Overture / Prologue (1990) / Musical 'Mamma Mia.'

"I've already told a few of you about the very first time I heard this selection. It's not how the movie and theatre performances begin, but I find it both shockingly stunning and delightful!"

Several students laughed and cheered.

"All right, settle down! I'm going to tell it," laughed Mary Beth. "I was in Las Vegas, and one of the shows I wanted to see was 'Mamma Mia,' which was riding the wave of its record-breaking engagement at the Mandalay Bay Theatre. We were lucky to get front-row seats right in the back of the orchestra pit. We thought, 'Go big or go home!'

"Before the show began, we were talking with a cute young lady down in the orchestra pit, and she was asking where we were from, if we were having a nice trip, etc. She seemed very happy and friendly. As the show got ready to start, things quieted down, and she turned around and said, 'I hope you enjoy this!'

"The next thing I heard was this huge sound of the first notes of this Overture! I almost jumped out of my seat! This nice young lady was actually the conductor and was having a ball! She looked over her shoulder and laughed out loud at our reaction!"

Mary Beth watched this incredible group of talented friends of all ages, excited, laughing, and having such a good time. She thought, *"This is just the reaction we want for our flash mob presentation! It's our big opportunity to show what we can do here in our Sea Crest Lighthouse Community."*

She was delighted as she reminded them, "All right, just so you know, I saw on YouTube that some of the comments verified that people in the theatre jump when they hear the start of this Overture, so don't get too carried away! I'm just like everyone else.

"This will lead into 'Dancing Queen' and 'Mamma Mia.' Looking around, I think most of you know the steps we learned for 'Dancing Queen.' I'll have some tips printed off for your review.

"These lead songs highlight extraordinary fun and energy. We've already practiced our routines when we perform with the superb choreography. We will produce an exciting flash mob.

"Our following flash mob selection will be Swing Dance. We'll dance to Glenn Miller's 'In the Mood.'

"As a reminder, we'll use the regular pattern we've learned previously for The Swing Dance.

1. Swing

2. Side Step
3. Rock Step
4. Double Rhythm
5. Partnering

"These are the basic moves you can embellish and have fun with. I've seen some of your creative movements, and they are awesome. Please feel free to enhance your artistic moves to show how talented and smooth our dance group has advanced. One of the silent auction prizes for the public to bid on is a set of dance lessons."

"Remember, anyone and everyone is welcome to join us on the dance floor or anywhere they have room.

"The third type of flash mob dance will be freestyle to Backstreet Boys – 'As Long As You Love Me.' The lyrics have a hopeful message with a touch of melancholy sorrow. It feels like no matter what, past or future, the love will be there."

As Mary Beth said those words, she had a brief moment where she sadly wondered, *"Will I ever dance with Zorro again. I saw him from across the room, and my world stood still. It's like the words of this song: I can't get you out of my head. I don't care what is written in your history."*

Mary Beth tried to ignore the feeling as she continued with the announcements, "To make things even more remarkable, we will have a changing room available for anyone who wants to wear a particular ensemble for the flash mob dances. The Sea Crest Inn has kindly volunteered to let us use one of their rooms as a dressing room. They have extra mirrors and lighting to help make it successful. We could bring our outfits beforehand to easily change before starting our dance routines.

"The Sea Crest Inn is conveniently located on the beach, only 3-4 minutes from the picnic area. They have a large women's lounge right off the dressing room, so it's another way to make our flash mob extraordinary. When we see Jimmy, the deejay, uncover his equipment, we should casually approach the dressing room.

"The following selection will be a flash mob Tango. Many of us have learned and loved the various Tango dances. It's one of our most popular dance classes, and we know routines for several songs. However, we've selected Al Pacino's Tango Dance from 'Scent of a Woman.' It's a classic and hands down favorite of our group.

"I must confess that Maggie has a surprise for us to dance to, but she hasn't shared that with me yet. We're all excited about our opportunity to create a flash mob. Remember, it's a surprise!"

Chapter Forty-Three

Maggie called Mary Beth, "Hi, I'm just checking to see if your silent auction meeting is today."

"I'm on my way out the door for it now. Would you like to come?" she replied.

"Not necessary, but I wondered how the items are progressing.

"It's looking good. So far, I have a set of dance lessons at The Sea Crest Dance Studio. They can pick any classes they'd like.

"The committee will fill me in on all their auction items. I'll let you know."

A few minutes later, Mary Beth met with the group. "Hello. Congratulations, I understand you're doing great with the donated auction items."

"Thanks for coming, Mary Beth," answered Linda. "I have the list right here."

"First, we have 'Yoga with Goats.' It's for two friends who love goats and have a sense of humor and a flexible body."

"Next, dinner for two at The Sea Crest Restaurant.

"Two-night stay at The Sea Crest Inn.

"Three surfing lessons with surfing champion Kate Jensen

"Your choice for a set of dance lessons at The Sea Crest Dance Studio.

"An overnight stay at the top of The Sea Crest Lighthouse.

"Scuba dive package to the site of the wreck of The Sea Crest Schooner.

"Night of bowling for you and your friends: 10 lanes, family, work team, scouts, club, church group?

"Cooking or baking lessons at Scrumptious Delights

"Crochet or knitting lessons at the Whimsical Yarnovers Shop.

"Horseback ride along the beach.

"Large wicker basket with products from The Sea Crest Boutique.

"Wicker basket with best seller books and audible books from The Sea Crest Book Nook.

"Large basket with French coffee press, with various coffee plus designer tea pot and variety of teas from The Tea Café.

"One-week rental for a bike at the beach.

"Deep Sea Marlin Fishing Excursion for two.

"Pickle ball lessons and/or court time – The Sea Crest Recreation Center.

"Surfboard – The Sea Crest Surf's-Up Shop.

"Guided tour of the Coast Guard Cutter that was patrolling the Sea Crest Coastline for smugglers.

"Matchmaker services – Call Abbie to arrange for service (with her contact number).

"The Sea Crest Lighthouse Series, complete set of books, by Carolyn Court."

Chapter Forty-Four

Antonio and Mary Beth called a meeting with their team to discuss the rules and procedures for the scavenger hunt.

Antonio stepped forward, "Hello, everyone. We want to thank you for your help in this fundraising effort for the Sea Crest Museum. This is mainly a brainstorming session to see how everything will fit together for a successful day of fun and meeting our financial goals."

Mary Beth added, "We have another support team working hard to develop this event's food and drink angle. I understand that various businesses have donated much of the food and drink that will be sold during the day or used at the seafood and BBQ picnic."

She smiled as she said, "Our blue crab vendors have agreed to donate a number of these unique crabs for the recipes of stuffed crabs and for the picnic. We are so lucky to have access to these colorful crabs. They live in coastal water areas from Nova Scotia, Canada, to South America. They are iconic in the waters of Maryland and Virginia, thriving in the Chesapeake Bay.

"The blue crabs have also been known to stow away on ship ballasts and shown up in the countries of Greece, Turkey, Italy, Israel, and Egypt. They are welcome to have the crustaceans as a delicious food and income."

One of the dancers asks, "What is a ballast?"

Antonio responded, "I'll take this one. It's anything, usually water, that stabilizes a boat. It's key for a safe trip. And I'd like to add, those blue crabs have shown up in many ports of the Mediterranean Sea."

He promptly stopped and shrugged as he stared helplessly at Mary Beth. "I have no idea how I know that, but I like it. It seems familiar for some strange reason."

Mary Beth saw he was amazed and smiled, "That's a good sign."

Antonio smiled and agreed, "Now, let's see what else needs to be discussed today." He looked at his notes and continued. "It appears like the silent auction is really picking up speed. I think the items that have been donated will bring in a nice sum."

Mary Beth looked at her notes and smiled. "Well, it seems Mary O'Hara, Maggie Jensen's mom, and Katherine Walsh, Kate Jensen's mom, will be in charge of our bake sale. We couldn't have two better choices. They are great!

"I've been close friends with those families since we were kids. Let me tell you, they know how to bake. I believe they are having a get-together later this afternoon if any of you are interested in making baked goods for sale or submitting a pie for the contest."

Antonio cut in, "Do they need someone to sample the food? I want to volunteer if that position is available."

Everyone laughed.

"Well," explained Mary Beth as she laughed. "It looks like they've got plenty to help with the baking. As of last night, I know they were talking it up. They had them signed up for cookies, pies, cakes, brownies, and fudge. Of course, the banana bread, tea rings, pumpkin bread, and zucchini bread are all being made, too."

She paused before she said, "You know, I didn't hear anything about needing someone to sample any of it."

Another big laugh, while Antonio looked sad and forlorn at Mary Beth.

"However, I did hear of someone needing to judge the pies tomorrow. They must find the best pie to award the blue ribbon to. I think you'll be perfect!"

Antonio blushed as he grinned and said, "I accept!"

Everyone clapped and congratulated him on his new appointment.

Antonio shut his notebook and announced, "I think my job here is done. I've accomplished my goal." He smiled good-naturedly and waved goodbye as the meeting broke up.

Antonio said, "These people are great, aren't they Mary Beth? I've never enjoyed a Scavenger Hunt this much before."

Mary Beth clapped her hands as she kidded him, "Antonio, how do you know? We might be terrible at planning a Scavenger Hunt, but now we know. You're just in it for the pie!"

He put his arm around her as they left the meeting without even thinking about it. Five steps later, once they got outside in the sunny light of day, it dawned on him what he'd just done. Antonio abruptly stopped, and as Mary Beth turned toward him, he gently held her in a dance move.

However, the feelings that flooded over him caused him to stumble. He let go of her so suddenly that he almost dropped her. Then he brusquely tried to catch her but only grabbed her hand. His notebook flew, and his knee buckled as he dropped to one knee in front of her in the middle of the sidewalk.

People around them started clapping. *"Good grief! Yes, it looks like I'm proposing!"*

Mary Beth knew he was floundering as she knelt beside him and softly said, "I'll have to take a rain check, but for now, I'll say 'Yes.' She raised her head, looked lovingly in his eyes, and said, 'Oui!'

"What?"

"I mean 'Yes'!" she smiled. "I'm sorry I ruined your proposal."

The crowd of onlookers was chanting, "Kiss! Kiss! Kiss!'

Antonio finally smiled and whispered, "Must we give the people what they want?"

With that, they rose together. He took his Chanel dream girl in his arms and gently kissed her. She raised her head and saw the love in his eyes. What she felt was shocking. Now he embraced her and slowly kissed her for real. For the first time in her life, she kissed him back.

The small group that had accumulated started clapping and cheering.

Chapter Forty-Five

"Well," Antonio murmured as they slowly picked up their notebooks and Mary Beth's handbag. "That was surprising!"

"Yes, to say the least."

Antonio turned to her and said, "Thank you for covering for me. That was very kind."

Mary Beth was shaking inside, but she pulled herself together enough to make light of the kisses. "Antonio, I hope things don't get weird between us now that we're engaged."

He smiled as they walked. "I think we did all right back there. You were great. I'm unsure what happened to me, but I'm glad you were with me."

"I feel the same."

Mary Beth knew that song that would really haunt her now.

Every little thing that you have said and done
Feels like it's deep within me
I can't get you out of my head

Chapter Forty-Six

The DEA and FBI planned to be on full alert for this Scavenger Hunt. They figured the smugglers at the top of the gang were unhappy with the drug bust, resulting in the big guys feeling this was a considerable loss.

Maggie called a meeting to address the possible threat to the Scavenger Hunt. "We need to be on full alert during this Scavenger Hunt to avoid any collateral damage at all costs."

Bill said, "Yes, but look at the huge opportunity we have to capture these guys. The three smugglers who threatened us at gunpoint have suffered a huge loss. Rest assured, they are going to retaliate during this Scavenger Hunt."

Maggie agreed, "We have to think like they would and prepare to act to safely stop them from harming anyone today. Let's make a foolproof plan that will work for us. Let's brainstorm! The floor is open to any and all ideas."

One of the DEA agents offered, "If I were the smugglers, I would know my higher-ups were gunning for me. I'd also know that there is no money or drugs to repay them to save my life. There is no reason to think we'll be alive, so I'd want to stay with the crowds of people at the Scavenger Hunt for cover. I think they're going to be here today."

Another one agreed, "Yes, they've got nothing to lose and everything to gain by mingling with the crowd. In fact, I think they might join the Scavenger Hunt as protection, too."

Maggie said, "Yes! We should set up a sting operation at the entrance to the game, where they sign in and officially start. We need to set up some cameras to get a headshot of every member of every team that arrives to play. Nothing easily visible, but a strong enough lens to capture their face.

"Since everyone who plays will be awarded an engraved brick, we'll need an ID card with the player's correct legal name.

"Most players will be taking pictures and photos to submit with several of the answers to the clues; that would be a regular thing we must do to keep the game fair and honest. The smugglers can't refuse, or it will draw attention to them and send up a red flag. We'll have the entire entrance to the Scavenger Hunt, manned by undercover agents.

"Remember that our objective isn't only to catch the local smugglers hiding from the big guys who took the significant loss. Still, we must take advantage of the opportunity to capture the big guys. The guys at the top of the food chain, so to speak.

"We must have our witnesses hidden somewhere for safety and have them with the apparatus to ID the men who threatened them at gunpoint."

One of the agents suggested, "Maybe we could have signs posted that no guns are allowed at the Scavenger Hunt."

Someone else said, "Another tool we can use is to offer free drinks to all entrants to the game. The containers should have something (cans or glasses) that will make it easy to hold fingerprints. We'd need a system so we could have a collection of all questionable strangers.

"We will also have their prints on the returned Scavenger Hunt clue sheet with some answers. Example: Some of the clues require a number. How many bricks are along the front step of the Sea Crest Church?"

Maggie closed by saying, "Great ideas! Thanks, we'll set up to meet all these requirements and arrest these smugglers!"

Chapter Forty-Seven

The smugglers were also planning what to do to stay alive after the drug bust! They were really infuriated now. "I never dreamed those guys would fall asleep with 41 bales of narcotics worth $41 million US dollars. We're in such trouble."

"I know the big guy has put a contract out on us. We won't last five minutes out on the water. We need to stay hidden. I mean, really hidden."

"I doubt he'll have the guys looking for us along the Sea Crest Coastal area. Especially with the Drug Enforcement Administration, Federal Bureau of Investigation, The United States Coast Guard, and Sea Crest Police in the area. I'm pretty sure that stupid Scavenger Hunt thing will keep them from killing us in broad daylight if they see us."

"Yeah! They won't be able to do anything to us with all the collateral damage. In this case, the injury inflicted on something other than an intended target would be super high. We're talking specifically about civilian casualties. The crowds might be the safest place for us to hang out."

"All right, the Scavenger Hunt starts tomorrow morning. Should we get an entry form and play their stupid game? It would keep us occupied and make us look like regular guys."

"Okay, we might as well try to get a good night's sleep and ensure we arrive at the entrance by the start time."

Chapter Forty-Eight

The smugglers may be getting a good night's sleep. However, the two other people who were actually running the Scavenger Hunt were getting anything but a good night's sleep.

Antonio lay awake staring at the ceiling tiles of his room at the Coast Guard Medical Center. *"What is going on with me? Every time I close my eyes, I relive that kiss! I hope I'm not really married in real life. If I was, somebody should have told me. What am I going to do? I'm actually afraid to recover from my amnesia! I want to be with Mary Beth!"*

Across town, Mary Beth was also having her own sleepless version of the 'Ground Hog Day Syndrome.' She couldn't stop recreating the fantastic afternoon with Antonio. Every time she drifted off to her dreamy proposal and the unbelievable kiss, it was hard to stop turning it over in her mind.

"What does it all mean? Does Antonio have feelings for me? Why do I seem to feel like I'm falling in love with him? I don't know anything about him except that I'm deeply drawn to him in a new and important way.

"I want him to feel the same, but it's very scary that he doesn't know what's happening with his brain or heart.

"What if he is already involved with someone else? He has no idea what his ties are, and although he may care for me, it may only go as deep as a lovely friend to hang out with (and propose to?) (and kiss to end all kisses?).

"I'm afraid to care any deeper than I do because it will break my heart if he doesn't feel the same way when he recovers. But why? I just met him. It's crazy! How can I explain my feelings for Antonio when I had such a strong reaction to Zorro at the Masquerade Ball?

"What on earth is going on with me? Do I fall for every guy who comes into my life?

"Oh no, I have to get some sleep! The Scavenger Hunt is in the morning!"

At the same time, Antonio was getting desperate. He called Doctor Lewis and left a message: "Hello Doctor, this is John Doe or Antonio. I need to see you as soon as possible. Early in the morning before the Scavenger Hunt would be necessary, if at all possible. This was an emergency of the highest order."

Early the following day, Doctor Lewis arrived to see Antonio. "It looks like you've had a breakthrough. Can you tell me what happened yesterday?"

Antonio explained, "Well, the day started out fine. Very good. However, I was with Mary Beth, and things were going very well until I stumbled and half fell against her. When I turned to move away from her, I almost embraced her like we were dancing. Of Course, it startled me, and I started to lose my balance and fall. I grabbed her hand to keep from falling further.

"The result was that I bent down on one knee, with her hand in my hand, like I was purposing. A small crowd gathered around, excited that I was proposing, so Mary Beth whispered that she may need a rain check, but she'd say Yes. Then she looked into my eyes and said, 'Oui.'

"I said 'what?' Because it recalled something so familiar that it really threw me.

"She said, 'Yes'.

"Everyone cheered.

"Then they started yelling 'Kiss,' 'Kiss,' 'Kiss.'

"So, I looked into her eyes and said some idiotic things about whether we should give them what they want. That referred to a joke we had spoken about earlier in the day. She was being so pleasant and appealing, plus she smelled so good. The Chanel was undeniable, and I couldn't resist her. That's when I kissed her. Can you believe it? I kissed Mary Beth!"

"What did she do?" asked the doctor.

"Well, she looked into my eyes, and I kissed her again. I mean a real kiss. And I'm pretty positive that she kissed me back!

"I could just die. I have no idea if I'm already married or not."

The doctor asked, "When it was over, how did Mary Beth act?"

"Well, she smiled and said, 'Antonio, I hope things don't get weird between us now that we're engaged.'

"I think she was trying to be sweet and didn't want me to be embarrassed."

"Well, that's good because you guys made the front page of the Sea Crest Newspaper."

Chapter Forty-Nine

This was just about when Maggie sat down with a cup of coffee and reached for her morning paper. Staring her in the face was a beautiful half-page picture of two of her best friends, looking positively smitten with each other.

Yes, Antonio, aka Philip, was down on one knee with Mary Beth's hand in his. Maggie looked carefully at this unbelievable turn of events and thought, *"I think Mary Beth is actually surprised, maybe even shocked."*

However, earlier this morning, Doctor Lewis had been the first to see the wedding proposal picture announcing the impending nuptials.

He had heard Antonio's desperate plea for 'Help' in the message he left. The doctor was eager to see him and went immediately. But he stopped dead in his tracks when he entered the Medical Center lobby and saw the newsstand. He was tempted to buy all the papers but decided to find out how Mary Beth acted after the event.

The cell phone picture was taken by an onlooker, and the caption directed the public to his video that was posted online.

The doctor promptly went to the post and watched the scene unfold before him. *"This is very telling on so many levels."*

Chapter Fifty

Mary Beth saw Antonio as she approached the entrance to the Scavenger Hunt. She didn't want him to know she'd tossed and turned all night. *"I'll try to act normal. Along with his memory loss, he might not remember our kisses."*

She greeted him with a happy smile, "Hi there, Mr. Pie Eater. Are you ready for this?"

Antonio knew he'd have to face her this morning and dreaded it. So, he was unprepared for how pretty she looked. Without thinking about it, he naturally took her hand. Then, feeling stupid, he turned and changed the action like he was shaking her hand.

"Sorry, sometimes I don't know how to act around you," he whispered.

Mary Beth smiled and said, "Well, since we're engaged, I think you're safe to take my hand."

He just laughed. "You always make me feel great, even when it's awkward. I love that about you. Whoops, there I go again. Those Freudian slips are awful. I'm sorry."

Mary Beth said, "Well, you're one of the most likable guys I've ever met, and I remember everything from my past or lack thereof. So, relax. I think you're great! No worries."

Now, embarrassed, she thought, *"All right, stop talking!"*

"I'm so happy we're doing the Scavenger Hunt together," Antonio said. *"However, I don't know if you'll even talk to me when you see that engagement picture on the newspaper's front page."*

Chapter Fifty-One

Several teams were gathered at the entrance to the Scavenger Hunt. They were given instructions as they lined up to get their official entry sheet with all the clues. The adults showed their IDs, and the children needed an adult to accompany them throughout the game.

Antonio was the first to address the gathering players, "Welcome to Sea Crest's First Annual Scavenger Hunt. We are honored to dedicate this as a fundraiser for the new Sea Crest Museum. You will hopefully learn some exciting and interesting things about our beautiful lighthouse community.

"Since this is not a timed event, we believe each team will come up with a sheet full of correct answers. We'd still like to honor everyone on your team for coming out to support the museum. Each person will have a special brick engraved with your legal name in that spirit. When our walkway is completed, the bricks will be placed as the pathway leading into the new Sea Crest Museum. Even families with several players each will have their names on bricks to commemorate as a contributor to building our museum. This is our wonderful community working together to honor our past. Thank you all."

Mary Beth smiled as she gave the instructions at the sign-up tent. "When you sign in, you'll be given your official entry sheet with all the clues.

"Adults need to show their ID. All children need to be accompanied by an adult throughout the game. Please print the names of all those on your team. First and last names, please. These will be engraved on your pathway brick.

"We have an easy way to log your answers as you proceed through the layout. You are encouraged to click a picture with your phone or tablet. That will save having to write or draw all the answers. Please log your cell number to the space on the sign-in sheet. You can send us a picture or text us to ask if this is correct. If you need medical help or have lost an item, please call or text us."

Antonio said, "We decided to borrow an idea from the golfers. Do we have any golfers here today?"

They all cheered and gave each other high fives.

"Well, you'll recognize where we're going with this. We'll start with a shotgun design similar to the golf start, which offers a distinctive approach to organizing the tournament, where all players simultaneously start their scavenger hunt from one of three locations. Your entry sheets will have your team's start location with your first clue. It will direct you to start near the Sea Crest Beach, the Sea Crest Church, or the Sea Crest Cemetery.

"We have about five minutes before we start, so once you're signed in, you're welcome to have some refreshments donated by the Sea Crest Lighthouse. Help yourself."

Mary Beth stepped up again to say, "This Scavenger Hunt is just the kick-off of today's fund-raiser celebration. Take advantage of the beach, and remember to be safe around the water.

"We will have a surfer show this afternoon at 3:30. When the Scavenger Hunt ends. The surfer's motto is 'You Can't Stop the Waves, But You Can Learn to Surf.'"

Just about this time, Jeffrey Williams found the person he was looking for. However, the person had been aware of him for at least five minutes. She'd tried to avoid him during the opening of the Scavenger Hunt event. She was here to learn all she could about the people's history in Sea Crest and didn't want any unwanted attention.

Meanwhile, Mary Beth continued to address the growing crowd. "We have the silent auction set up throughout the day in the white tent areas. We've got lots of super nice items to bid on."

That's when Jeffrey Williams strolled over to Abigail and said sternly, "Hello. Speaking of the silent auction, I believe you are in possession of my list of what I'm bidding on."

"What pray tell are you talking about?" she replied airily. "I'd be embarrassed to admit to your trivial bid for a stay at the Sea Crest Inn or your insignificant bid for a dinner at the Sea Crest Restaurant. I couldn't care less where you sleep or what you eat! However, those paltry bids won't even pay for the tip!"

Jeffery was suddenly interested in showing her just how rude he thought she was. "Oh, I'm sorry, I thought I was talking to a normal person who had something of mine. I assumed you'd want to return the item to the rightful owner; however, I stand corrected. I'm actually dealing with a thief. You just want to make sure you bid higher. Well, it's always nice to know the moral fiber of your competition."

"Are you talking from your experience as a shoplifter or a pickpocket? Perhaps you ran into me and tried to steal my computer yesterday. You're lucky I didn't have my pepper spray with me."

Attorney Jeffery Williams was definitely not going to let her get away with that remark. "You'll see me in court, young lady!" he promised as he turned away.

He wondered what his blood pressure was registering as he mentally prepared his opening statement for the future demise of his wicked adversary. *"Looks can only carry you so far, Sweetie! Yikes, where did that come from?"*

He walked back toward the starting entrance of the Scavenger Hunt just in time to see Antonio join Mary Beth and add, "Later this afternoon, we'll have our seafood and BBQ pot-luck picnic. Lots of great food. A couple of our sponsors will be grilling special regional recipes from Upstate New York. One popular marinated specialty is called Spiedies, and it's been famous in the Tri-City Area for decades. The other is their famous Marinated Grilled Chicken. These will both be set up with special BBQ grills over by the white tents!"

"What is the Tri-City Area of New York?"

"That's the three cities, Binghamton, Endicott, and Johnson City. The last two are villages, but they lie along the southern part of New York State. They have hot air balloons, kite flying festivals, and celebrations along the Chenango and Susquehanna riverfronts. Spiedies and fried chicken are always popular foods available for all occasions.

"Another specialty is a Thanksgiving Turkey Dressing to die for. We'll have special items from all around. In fact, I will be a judge for the best pie. Somebody's going to win a blue ribbon."

"I hear they are having a pie eating contest, a bake sale, and a chili cook-off.

Mary Beth finished, "We'll have music and a snap-together dance floor that covers the sand on the beach. We'd love everybody to help celebrate the new Sea Crest Museum with us."

Meanwhile, three real smugglers mingled with the crowd as they neared the sign-up table.

They had a decision to make. One of them commented to his fellow smuggler, "Well, I don't think it will matter if we use our real IDs to sign up. We don't have any choice in how they've set this up."

"I know what you mean. We need to stay with the other players and seem as normal as possible. In fact, I think I'll have some of that coffee they've got up there."

"Let's get signed up, get our clue sheet, and keep our eyes open for the drug dealers that are after us. We'll be lucky if we survive this day."

Three undercover men watched them from the Sea Crest Inn lookout when they approached the sign-in table. Charley, Bill, and Jack each zoomed in with their binoculars and recognized they were the smugglers who had threatened them at gunpoint. Charley had spotted them when they wandered into the entrance area.

Charley reported to the other agents in the area. "We've got the three smugglers on our video on our binoculars. They are at the table right now. It looks like one of them is getting coffee. Call down to Antonio and make sure they save his coffee cup if he drops it in the trash."

Bill added, "See what names they each signed into the game with. What's on their ID cards?"

Jack also reminded them, "Do not apprehend or show suspicion in any way. These guys are in big trouble because they fell asleep, costing them millions. They have a target on their back as an example for the rest of the cartel organization. Don't make stupid mistakes. We're searching for the big guy. The boss. "

The DEA agent stationed by the entrance was watering the hanging baskets overflowing with 'wave' petunias. He wore sunglasses, and his position allowed him to move around and observe everyone. He'd received a signal about the info of the three smugglers at the sign-in table. He'd keep them under surveillance and help with any apparent problems that came up.

He also observed three men wandering around who didn't seem to fit in the crowd. He alerted the Sea Crest Inn agents to the possibility that they might be a match for the big guys. Or at least a higher level in the smuggler's organization.

The next couple of hours went along smoothly. The Scavenger Hunt was turning into a big success.

The second sighting of the suspicious guys appeared right on target. They were undoubtedly following the three local smugglers, waiting for a chance to take them out.

As the Scavenger Hunt winded down, there was a large influx of food items. The bake sale was well underway, with many sales to help with the event's fundraising goals. Michael and James Jensen had a giant tally board to mark the advance of the money as it came in.

Early afternoon was ideal for the ever-popular chili cook-off. People milled around and tasted and voted for their favorite chili. The judging categories for the chili are as follows:

'Traditional red chili,' – aka – bowl of red, usually has a smoky flavor, which can be achieved with the right combination of fresh and dried chiles and peppers. It often has a bacon and beef base originating in the Southwest.

'Chili verde'- green chili is made with tender pork, tomatillo, and roasted pepper sauce. It usually includes jalapeno, anaheim, and poblano peppers. Often served with crunchy tortilla chips, lime wedges, or maybe even a dollop of sour cream.

'Homestyle chili' is the only category that permits the use of 'fillers,' such as beans and pasta.

'Salsa' – combines tomatoes, onions, and chili peppers. Often used for chips, tacos, and many Mexican dishes. Dip hot or cold. Adjust the spices for a hot-mild flavor. Originated as long ago as the Aztec and Inca societies.

Later in the afternoon, Mary Beth and Antonio were leisurely strolling, waiting for the Scavenger Hunt applications to be processed. Mary Beth glanced at her watch and exclaimed, "Oh No! The best pie contest! We're going to be late. Hurry!"

"Wait just a minute. You don't have to come. I'm sure you have more pressing obligations to fulfill," Antonio laughed, nudging her away.

Mary Beth teased, "Oh no! You're not getting out of this so easy; I wouldn't miss this for the world."

"What do you mean? I was practically forced into accepting that thankless job. I didn't see anyone else with their hand up, did you?"

"You were practically begging to do it."

"Why do you have to come, anyway? I have important work to do. I don't need you looking over my shoulder, trying to 'scare me'!"

"Oh yeah"? she laughed. She tried to think of something outrageous to say. After a minute, she started to giggle.

Antonio suspiciously asked, "What's so funny?"

She laughed, "Well, I can't wait to see you......."

Now he was laughing, "What? You can't wait to see me ... what?"

Mary Beth held her stomach as she tried to catch her breath. At last, she said in a high, squeaky voice, "I can't wait to see you eat the blueberry pie and walk around all day with a blue tongue!"

"Well, thanks a lot!" He laughed. "You're a riot!"

They were still laughing when they got to the location for the best pie contest.

Chaplain O'Reilly was also there to judge the delicious pies. However, he was also considering their behavior at the moment. "Good afternoon, Mary Beth and Antonio." He said sternly. "It's so nice to see you together again. I hope you're behaving yourselves today. It was disgraceful to find you laughing together in the cemetery yesterday."

The Chaplain skipped a beat before he burst out laughing. "Oh, it does my heart good to see you two so much in love. You make a lovely couple, and I'd like to offer my services when you're ready to tie the knot. I think you're perfect for each other."

"Oh no," Antonio was quick to set this straight. "That was a mistake. I stumbled, and my knee gave out. I caught Mary Beth's hand to keep from falling. When I ended up on a bent knee holding her hand, the people around us thought I was proposing. It was all a mistake. It wasn't real!"

"Oh, I find that hard to believe. You may have amnesia, but I know true love when I see it. I'm never wrong. Besides, I saw the video online. It sure looks real to me."

Mary Beth couldn't believe her ears. "What video? Is it online?"

Antonio shook his head as he gently explained, "Apparently, one of the spectators was filming the whole thing. He also sent a picture to the newspaper with information on where to watch the video of us. I haven't seen it."

"What are we supposed to do now?"

"I called Doctor Lewis last night because I couldn't sleep. I was very upset about our kiss."

Mary Beth took a short, painful look into his eyes as a tear rolled down her cheek.

"Oh, no!" Antonio whispered. "It's not what you think. I kept wondering if I was married or had another fiancé or girlfriend. What if I have kids. How can I fall in love with you if I'm in love with somebody else."

Mary Beth was still speechless.

"Well, it will all work itself out. At least, this proves what a good heart you have. It's good to know there are still guys around who honor their marriage vows, and now I know that marriage means something precious to you.

"I have somewhere I need to be right now, so I guess I'll see you later, Antonio. Bye, Chaplain O'Reilly."

Chapter Fifty-Two

Mary Beth went to her real estate office and locked the door behind her. She sat in solitude for an hour and contemplated her future. *"The problem is I've never been in love before."*

Zorro

Now, I could fall in love with this disappearing Zorro guy if I ever meet him again.

I was attracted to him from across the room.

He likes Zorro.

What a dancer!

He knows French.

He'd make a good living as a disappearing magician.

He felt great as he was holding me to dance.

Antonio

Now, I feel like I'm already falling in love with Antonio, aka John Doe.

He has a great sense of humor.

He trusts me – He didn't press charges on the three guys that clobbered him.

He likes my perfume

He respects the vows of marriage and hopes to figure out if he's involved with another girl or if he has kids.

He loves pie! At that one, she smiled. *I hope he ends up with a bright blue tongue!*

He loves history and likes to plan Scavenger Hunts with a French flare.

He knows lots of stuff about pirates.

He's a great DEA agent who has worked with Maggie before.

I like being around him.

I loved our kiss, and I kissed him back.

I keep playing that Back Street Boys song, 'As Long As You Love Me,' repeatedly.

Mary Beth was confused. Both men had qualities that she loved.

That's just great. First, I have no men that I think I could fall in love with. Then, in a matter of days, I had two. I felt I was on the verge of falling in love with them.

What if it's all one-sided? What if I never see Zorro again? How can I feel so much for both men at the same time? Good Grief! I kissed Antonio! I dreamed of both men and don't know how I can feel this much for them!

Chapter Fifty-Three

The aroma was heavenly as the BBQ and grilling proceeded to fill the air with their tasty goodness.

The bake sale was a real money maker as the public could purchase their favorite treats. The pies were a big hit, as usual. Since Kate's mom won the first prize for her blueberry pie, she had the honor of having the most expensive price tag on her pies.

Mary Beth asked Antonio to show her his blue tongue, and he refused with great humor. "No way! I think you are going too far with your demands!" He laughed.

"Well, I certainly don't think you were qualified to judge anything that tasty. Maybe next year you can judge the sauerkraut eating contest. That's more your speed."

"I heard that Kate's brother Connor and Chaplain O'Reilly entered."

"Yes, and Connor gave me a run for my money. He came in a close second. Boy, can that kid eat!"

"Speaking of eating, do you see all our food for this potluck picnic?"

"Yes, and I'm half starved. It's hard work judging the best pie contest," Antonio answered.

"I want to go for some of those blue crabs. I've had them before, but both vendors have different recipes for their crab cakes. I want to sample both of them today and see which one I enjoy the most."

"That sounds like a splendid idea. I think I'll join you."

"I wouldn't have it any other way! I have to keep an eye on you. I never know when you'll try to sneak away and try to get a tattoo," she stated in her best school-teacher voice.

"Well, I'll have to keep an eye on you and make sure you don't get yourself kidnapped," he said thoughtfully.

"Since this is an 'all you can eat' picnic, I vote we get started."

The time flew, and everyone had all the seafood they could possibly want.

Chapter Fifty-Four

It looked like Jimmy, the deejay, was loitering around the boxes with heavy material draped over them. He casually started to remove the cover from his sound equipment.

The flash mob people proceeded to roam around, and soon, they were approaching their various positions for the flash mob.

When Jimmy gave the loud, stunning sound of the 'Mamma Mia Overture, ' people jumped, and the dancers ran out to take their first steps on the first flash mob ever in the Sea Crest Coastal Area.

The big guy smugglers almost pulled their weapons, thinking, "Wow! That sounds like gunfire!"

The audience was stunned, to say the least. After a moment, they began to stand up and cheer with sheer delight.

Before drawing his gun, the smuggler leader briefly realized it was 'only music.' He yelled to the other guys with him, "This could be the distraction we were waiting for."

His buddy said, "Hey, Boss, we can't start something here!"

At hearing that, Mary Beth jumped across and danced right up in his face, singing at the top of her lungs. When Antonio realized she was in harm's way, he immediately flew to her side. He danced, waved his arms before the smuggler, and pulled the dancing Mary Beth out of danger. They completely confused both smugglers and transported them into a mixed-up mess.

A second later, another pair danced over, started singing, and carried on to the music. By the time 'The Mamma Mia Overture' was finished, the big guy smugglers were separated by a myriad of dancing fanatics.

Maggie and the DEA knew what had just happened and took full advantage of the situation. Maggie appeared before the lead smuggler and immediately sang and danced a perfect rendition of 'Dancing Queen' without missing a beat. Her FBI partner and a couple of other Drug Enforcement Agency agents had him surrounded. The audience was stunned, to say the least. After a moment, they began to stand up and cheer with sheer delight.

The dancers followed up with 'Mama Mia' (the third Abba selection). This kept the excitement going and added to the organized chaos. It was wild! The crowd didn't know if this was part of the plan, but with the start of 'Mama Mia,' the spectators and the dancing maniacs joined in singing their hearts out.

The local smugglers fled across the sandy beach when they noticed what was happening. However, that wasn't a perfect idea after all. Mary Beth quickly instructed the dancers to form a ring around the men and confuse them as they tried to escape. DEA and FBI agents came from out of nowhere and chased them into the pounding waves.

Some dancers kicked off their shoes and sandals and danced in the surf to prevent them from getting away. As a result, undercover agents from all branches of drug control surrounded the remaining smugglers.

Antonio spotted Mary Beth and could hardly contain himself with pride as he gave her a thumbs-up and yelled, "You guys were great!"

She smiled back and yelled back, "You too! Good job!"

The smugglers were soaked to the bone and gasping for breath. They looked like half-drowned rats as they stumbled out of the waves. The agents brought their life of crime to a sorry end as they showed their badges and arrested all six smugglers.

The delighted dancers clapped their hands and kept up with their singing and dancing with the change of dance as they jumped into the beginning of the Swing Dance selection, 'In the Mood!' The dancers were on fire with the complete routine that had been part of their dance lives for years but never this enthusiastically.

Antonio grabbed Mary Beth, "Are you okay?"

"Yes. Boy, that was something!"

"Yeah. And you, my dear, were spectacular. You are a superb dancer."

Amid all the mayhem, the deejay announced, "Well, when Sea Crest plans a flash mob, they don't mess around, do they?"

Everyone laughed, wondering exactly what had happened, but they loved the show.

Then Jimmy continued, "We'll have a small intermission while the authorities take out the 'Trash'!"

This got the crowd going, and everyone cheered and clapped as the smugglers were hauled to jail in the paddy wagon.

This was an ideal opportunity for the dancers to desert the dance floor and change into their outfits for 'The Tango,' part of the flash mob!

Jimmy continued with the Backstreet Boys 'As Long As You Love Me.' This was a pleasant choice for the crowd to enjoy. He called out, “This is for everyone. Come on up and give it a whirl.”

The lyrics spoke to Antonio’s heart as the harmonious notes flowed through the air. He couldn’t take his eyes off Mary Beth as he felt,

‘I’m leavin’ my life in your hands
Risking it all in a glance
I can’t get you out of my head
Don’t care what is written in your history

Well, that’s rich. I don’t know what my own history is.”

Mary Beth saw him thoughtfully gazing at her, and she desperately wanted to share a dance with him. *“I’m almost afraid to ask him. Will it be too forward for me? Will it change how great we are together?”* However, she prayed that he’d say yes, as she gently explained, “Antonio, anyone can join in these dances. I see that you’re an excellent dancer. Would you like to be my partner for this next dance?”

“I guess I could give it a shot. But I have something important to tell you first.”

Mary Beth braced herself for the worst but hoped for the best. “Okay,” she whispered.

“Well, I spoke to Maggie. She’s known me for a long, long time. I asked her if I was married. She said, ‘No, and I’ve never been married. It’s not even close. But she saw our front-page picture in the newspaper, watched the video, and thought it looked real.

“I told her I haven’t regained my whole memory, but I have strong feelings for you.

“I told her I’d remembered a few things but didn’t connect them to any face. It scares me. I feel something, but I don’t know what it is.

He continued, "Maggie told me I'll be surprised when I finish remembering everything. She said she knows something about my feelings and that I'm on the verge of a breakthrough and should relax and enjoy this time.

"Mary Beth," he continued. "I'm pretty mixed up about many of my feelings, but "Yes," I'd love to dance with you."

Mary Beth said, "Great. I'm scared, too, but I will take a chance on you. I have to change into another outfit, but can you wait a minute for me. Maggie said she has something special that our deejay will play for us dancers. It's a surprise for us, and she won't tell us what it is. However, she promised that we'll like it."

"Great, I don't know the routines, but of course, I'd love to dance with you."

"Wonderful," Mary Beth was filled with joy and didn't want to go anywhere. However, she knew she had to go change into another outfit. "I'll see you in a few minutes."

He whispered, reluctantly letting go of her hand, "I'll wait for you, Mary Beth."

Chapter Fifty-Five

As Mary Beth was dressing, she could hear the beautiful music of the tango, 'Scent of a Woman.' She took one long minute to look in the mirror and touch up her makeup as she got ready. There was a knock on her dressing room door.

"Hi, Mary Beth? It's Maggie. Open up."

As she turned to greet her friend, she saw what she held in her arms. "What are you holding? I already brought an outfit to change into."

"Mary Beth, I have something much more important for you to wear right now," Maggie said as she unzipped the hanging wardrobe bag.

Mary Beth was surprised. "Thanks, did you pick that up at the cleaners for me? How nice."

"No. This is part of the surprise I have for you. Please wear this costume. I brought the black bob wig and shoes you wore to the Masquerade at the Lighthouse."

"Why?" asked Mary Beth suspiciously. "I don't understand."

"Just please do it for me. It will mean so much to me. I didn't get your picture the other night and I love this outfit."

"Okay, did you bring the mask?"

"No, I don't want a picture of you in a mask. Hurry up, they're waiting for you!"

When she was ready, Mary Beth and Maggie walked across the courtyard toward the dance floor.

Mary Beth was surprised as she commented, "Oh, I thought I was the last one out, but where is everyone?"

There was no one else on the dance floor when she stepped onto it, and the music of 'The Spanish Tango' from the 'Zorro' movies began.

Antonio slowly stepped onto the floor and moved toward the flapper and Maggie. He looked ready to collapse as he realized it was Mary Beth.

She saw his distress and softly whispered, "Antonio, "Puis-je avoir cette danse?" (May I have this dance?)

He said 'Oui' and stepped onto the dance floor with her.

The scent of Chanel N°5, the flapper dress, the black bob wig, Mary Beth. He drew her into his arms and held her tight.

Mary Beth was in heaven, *"This is the best feeling in the world."*

He stopped dancing and drew her back at arm's length as he looked into her eyes. This was almost as much of a welcomed shock for Mary Beth as it was for him. She never dreamed Antonio, aka John Doe, was actually Zorro. *"This is the luckiest day of my life! I don't have to choose. I get them both!"*

They gazed into each other's teary eyes, and it all came flooding back to him. "Wow, this is a miracle," Antonio said in an emotional voice. "I'm remembering everything now."

It was like the whole rest of the world had disappeared to them.

"Mary Beth, I love you so much! May I kiss you for real now?"

"Of course. You're the only man I've ever kissed back," she laughed.

"I knew it!" He said as he kissed her for real!

Antonio said, "I knew I was falling in love with you, and for the record, you're the only woman I've ever proposed to."

Mary Beth smiled, saying, "I won't hold you to it, but if you mean it, I'll love you forever."

Antonio immediately held her hand and knelt down on one knee. "Mary Beth, I love you now, and I'll love you forever. Please marry me!"

Mary Beth looked at him with love as a tear rolled down her cheek. "Antonio, I love you dearly and I would love to marry you!"

They embraced as they kissed and felt like the two luckiest people on the face of the earth.

"Mary Beth, do you remember the items on the list for the silent auction?'

"Of course. Did you want to make a bid on something?"

"Well, it's up to you, but what if we won, 'An overnight stay at the top of The Sea Crest Lighthouse.' We could get married at the top and then stay overnight."

"That would be great!"

"Then we could take off for our honeymoon in Paris!" Antonio said. "But of course, I'd love our honeymoon anywhere you pick." He remembers, *"Grace talking about Mary Beth's love of Paris while stranded on the remote Tahiti Island."*

Mary Beth was absolutely delighted. "Wow, I love Paris. Our honeymoon there would be perfect, but I'll be happy anywhere with you."

Jimmy interrupted their plans by announcing, "Our Coast Guard Chaplain has requested an additional five minutes on the silent auction while our newly engaged couple decide if they want to bid on the night at the top of the Sea Crest Lighthouse."

Chaplain O'Reilly waved happily to them. *"I was sure they were in love, and I'm happy to be of service should the need arise."*

People from the seafood and BBQ picnic took their place on the dance floor as Mary Beth and Antonio made their way to the silent auction table.

"Wow, this will be a beautiful wedding," Antonio said, looking at the information on the overnight at the top of the lighthouse.

"Yes, it will be a dream come true. You know my friend Grace was stranded on an uninhabited Tahiti Island. She ended up getting married twice to the same man while she was there. Once onboard Chaplain O'Reilly's Coast Guard Cutter and once at the top of the Tahiti Lighthouse.

"That sounds wonderful. I'm so happy for her."

"Well, I know you didn't even know her, but she's wonderful."

"Let's make a bid on the overnight stay at the lighthouse, and I think I'll include a bid on the dinner for two at the Sea Crest Restaurant."

"Oh, Antonio, we have to bid on the "Large basket with French coffee press, with various coffee plus a designer Tea Pot & variety of teas from The Tea Café. That's where we met for High Tea. I loved that place!"

"All right, I guess we've bid on enough unless there's something else you'd like."

"No, I'm good," she laughed. "I'm so happy that you love me back. I was afraid it was all one-sided, but I just couldn't stop falling for you!"

They returned to the picnic area and waited to get the results of the silent auction. They were blessed to be the highest bidder on each item they bid on.

Chapter Fifty-Six

Chaplain O'Reilly needed to see this before he bounded forward to offer his services. "You may remember from the previous impromptu weddings I've completed that I'm ready, willing, and able to perform a lovely wedding at a moment's notice.

"I've watched you two over the past few days and observed kindness and caring develop while you fell in love."

"What?" gasped Mary Beth. "We didn't know anything about each other."

She let that outburst settle before she practically exploded, "I'm sure the only thing we were concentrating on was that Antonio needed to recover his memory! He had no feelings for me!"

"No," Antonio interjected with a laugh. "The first thing I thought was that you'd knocked me unconscious with a piece of driftwood. When I moaned and tried to turn over, You were there. You sure didn't look like a smuggler!"

Mary Beth protested, "You had a nerve, thinking I'd hurt you. I was trying to save you!"

Antonio laughed while he tried to get out, "Hurt me, Save me, 'Tomayto-tomahto.' I call them like I see them. I thought that a suspicious 911 phone call was the last straw. But you kept up the game until I heard the Coast Guard helicopter land."

"Well, you've got to be kidding me. After all I was doing for you."

"On your behalf, I remember you ripping your lace ruffle off your sundress and tying it around my wound to stop the bleeding. Thank you! It smelled of Chanel N°5, and it was marvelous!"

They were both laughing now. "Frankly," Antonio explained. "I don't know why you were even there. Dressed up in that sundress, with the breeze blowing through your hair. I couldn't stop looking at you!"

The Chaplain declared, "That's what I saw! Right there! The few times I've seen you together, you're delightful. The laughter and pure enjoyment that you display is amazing to watch. I think you're perfect for each other!"

"I think so, too," Antonio responded. It was starting to dawn on him that, *"I have a 'past' to explain to my new fiancée. I now remember spending days with Grace on the uninhabited island of Tahiti. Grace and Maggie are close, lifelong friends of Mary Beth, and I'd better share the recent facts with her."*

"What do you say if we talk with Doctor Lewis and get some guidance on proceeding? I have my complete memory back, but I'd like his opinion. I don't want to mess up the dream marriage of a lifetime because I didn't talk my love situation over with him."

"Of course, that seems like a positive step," agreed Mary Beth. "After all, Maggie has worked with you undercover for years. I don't know what, if anything, Doctor Lewis will come up with, but I'd also love his opinion."

Antonio asked, "Can I have a brief word with you, Chaplain, before we go?"

When they were alone, he asked, "Thanks for delaying the silent auction close until we could decide. That was very considerate of you."

"You're welcome. Anything I can do to help."

"Well, could you please see if we can arrange our wedding at the top of the lighthouse tomorrow? I also don't know, but I think I need to use my new legal name, Antonio."

"Yes, I can arrange the ceremony and have your marriage license."

"Great! I hope she still wants to marry me after our talk with Doctor Lewis," said Antonio nervously.

"I'm sure that won't be a problem," he replied. "She's been in love with you most of the time since she met you."

Chapter Fifty-Seven

A short time later, they arrived at Doctor Lewis' office. "Hello, Antonio and Mary Beth," he greeted them with a smile. "What can I do for you today?"

Antonio explained, "I've regained my memory!"

"Wonderful! I thought you were on the road to recovery soon. Very nice! I'm so glad!"

Antonio took Mary Beth's hand and continued, "I've asked Mary Beth to marry me for real this time. We have fallen in love during our time together, and Chaplin O'Reilly is prepared to marry us as soon as possible."

"Well, I must say, this is no surprise to me. I've been watching you both grow close and show the strong bond between you."

Mary Beth said, "I know Antonio has some job-related questions and past things that he wants to share with me, and we are asking for your opinion of where the line is drawn on building an honest, healthy future together based on what he knows and what I don't know."

She continued, "I'm not entirely sure why I would even be told something if it's Top Secret, but I want to be aware of anything important if it involves our future."

There was a tap on the door, and Maggie, Kate, and Grace entered the room.

"Hey, what are you guys doing here?" Mary Beth asked.

"Well, we heard that congratulations are in order for you," Maggie said as she hugged Mary Beth.

Kate said, "Yes, we're so happy for you."

When she hugged her, Grace had tears in her eyes and said, "I'm thrilled for both of you. Now, we have so much to tell you."

Then Grace also hugged Antonio, which Mary Beth was surprised at.

Maggie said, "Mary Beth, we have a top-secret story to tell you. We never would have been able to share this information with you if you weren't marrying Antonio."

Mary Beth looked apprehensive and said, "You guys are scaring me. What's the matter?"

Maggie said, "Mary Beth, we all love you, especially Antonio, but we will ask you to trust us. We will tell you what happened behind the scenes in Tahiti and why it's Top Secret."

Mary Beth said, "When I was in Tahiti? You guys were there too. What did I miss?"

Maggie said, "I'm going to hit the important high points. So, please let me recap these parts, and then you can ask questions. Okay?"

Mary Beth kissed Antonio and said, "I'm listening."

Again, Maggie said, "Mary Beth, you were the first to know Grace was going to Tahiti. You drove her to the airport. (No Problem).

"The next day, you got on a plane and followed her to Tahiti. (No Problem).

Antonio interrupted, "Mary Beth! You were in Tahiti?"

She shook her head and said, "Yes."

Antonio said, "Wow! That's why Chaplain O'Reilly said he saw you in Tahiti?"

She shook her head 'yes' again, and he kissed her again. "I love that!"

Maggie laughed sternly, "I will plow ahead with the story if you save your questions until the end.

"Now," Maggie continued, "Grace arrived in Tahiti, saw a little yellow pontoon plane, and asked for a ride (No problem).

"The pilot thought Grace was a drug smuggler trying to make a drug drop near the Tahiti Lighthouse. (Big Problem)

" The pilot was an undercover International Drug Enforcement operative named Philip, whom I'd known for years. He was working undercover at Tahiti and only spoke French to Grace. He took her up in the little yellow seaplane, which crashed on an uninhabited island. (Big Problem)

"Mary Beth, you came the 2nd day but didn't know Grace was missing yet."

"Kate and I came with the rest of the friends and family, who all arrived in Tahiti looking for Grace and an unknown pilot.

"Mary Beth and Philip survived for the next few days while we looked for them.

"Meanwhile, the drug cartel grew suspicious of Philip and his seaplane, and they were looking for him also.

"Kate picked Grace and Philip up as the US Coast Guard Search and Rescue pilot."

"Wait!" Mary Beth asked, "Kate. Did you pick up both Grace and this Philip pilot? I thought he drowned! They found his plane wrecked?"

"No, they were both alive and well," said Kate. "I took them to The US Coast Guard Cutter, and Maggie was onboard with Chaplain O'Reilly to greet us. Imagine our surprise when

Maggie ran up to greet her old undercover partner, Philip. It shocked us all."

"To keep Philip safe, he needed a new identity and a back story that he didn't survive. The Coast Guard found the yellow seaplane, totaled it, and left the remains on an uninhabited island for the drug cartel to find."

Maggie explained, "My good friend Philip was issued his new chosen name of Antonio."

Mary Beth turned to Antonio, who was observing her with such love that she felt she'd burst. "Is this who you are?"

Doctor Lewis said, "That's why his amnesia was such a problem on many levels. He had an alias as recently as a couple of months ago and was trying to recover. Mary Beth, one of the most important memory anchors was the Chanel N°5 scent that you wore. It was an important link to his time in France and his favorite perfume. It somehow grounded him in a good place."

Maggie repeated the warning that Antonio's former identity was top secret.

Antonio asked Mary Beth, "I know it's a lot to process. How are you feeling?"

She answered, "I love you so much. Probably in a deeper place in my heart because I know something wonderful about your past. The whole time you had amnesia, I knew nothing about your history. I hope to spend the rest of my life learning more with each day we are blessed with."

Antonio said, "Good. I was preparing to get down on my knee and ask you again."

They all laughed as they left Doctor Lewis' office.

Chapter Fifty-Eight

"I think the Scavenger Hunt and the Sea Crest Museum Fundraiser were a huge success," said Antonio. They were strolling along the beach, and the crowd was laying out blankets and beach chairs to watch the fireworks display.

"Let's sit over here and watch. Of course, there's not a bad seat in the whole coastal area," pointed out Mary Beth.

Antonio asked Mary Beth as they got situated, "I hope you're not planning on a long engagement. I think one day is plenty."

Mary Beth agreed, "That's long enough for me."

"Well, since we won the night at the top of the Sea Crest Lighthouse, let's arrange to have our wedding there tomorrow."

"Oh, here comes our favorite Chaplain," Mary Beth said as she flagged him down to join them.

Chaplain O'Reilly happily complied. "I'm so glad I found you. How did things go with Doctor Lewis?"

Antonio said, "They went fine. He also had Maggie, Grace, and Kate present to tell Mary Beth the Top Secret back story. I learned a couple of things also. I wondered why you told

Mary Beth she looked different than she did in Tahiti. And best of all, Mary Beth still agreed to marry me. I'm thrilled."

The Chaplain said, "That's great because you won the 'Stay at the Top of the Sea Crest Lighthouse. I just wanted you to know that I went ahead and made the arrangements for your wedding tomorrow, as you requested."

"That's wonderful. Oh, there are my parents," Mary Beth ran over to see them. "Mom, Dad, I wanted you to know I'm getting married tomorrow. We will have the Chaplain marry us at the top of the Sea Crest Lighthouse! Mom, I'd love to wear your wedding dress if the offer is still good."

"Of course, Dear. It's ready and waiting for you!

Antonio quickly joined them, and the parents congratulated them both. Apparently, Antonio had asked Mary Beth's father for her hand in marriage two days ago while she was getting her hair done. That's when her mom had gotten the beautiful wedding gown out of storage, just in case.

They had never seen their daughter in love before, and it was marvelous to see her so happy.

The fireworks started, and the light display was thrilling!

Chapter Fifty-Nine

Mary Beth gazed in the mirror at the happiest image of herself that she'd ever seen. Her blond hair was swept up with wisps of hair, framing it in soft tendrils that made her look like an angel. The gown had a long train, which would be added after she reached the lighthouse's top.

Kate, Maggie, and Grace had come to her parents' house to help her prepare. As they fussed and primped over every little detail, Kate said, "Aren't we the luckiest friends in the world? All of us married this year."

Mary Beth told them how special Antonio was to her on the short ride to the Sea Crest Lighthouse. They wrote a couple of lines of vows to tell how much they meant to each other.

As they arrived, they saw that the groom and the Chaplain were already waiting at the top for them. Mary Beth's family and friends joined them.

Mary Beth looked radiant as she walked to meet Antonio.

The Chaplain thought, *"These two are meant for each other, and they'll have a kind and fruitful life together. It's an honor and privilege to marry them."*

Antonio promised:

Mary Beth,
I will forever be there to laugh with you,
to lift you up when you're down,
and love you unconditionally.

Mary Beth promised:

Antonio,
I promise to encourage you,
and inspire you and to love you,
through good times and bad.

It was a perfect day for blessings for their vows at the top of the Sea Crest Lighthouse!

Keep reading for an excerpt from

Matchmaker or Troublemaker at the Sea Crest Lighthouse

The fifth book in

The Sea Crest Lighthouse Series

By Carolyn Court

Attorney Jeffrey Williams recovered from his collapse into the stranger beside the elevator doors. Their belongings were strewn around them on the Sea Crest Inn floor. He was the gentleman who created the fall in the first place as he lost his balance and grabbed her on the way to the floor. He tried to quickly pick up the scattered belongings. These included a laptop computer and a notebook opened to a page that read Matchmaker or Troublemaker.

He looked up into the face of the beautiful young woman, who turned angry as she instructed him to STOP! Jeffrey promptly set her laptop down at her rudeness and tossed the papers back onto the floor.

As he walked away, he thought, "No one talks to me like that." However, in haste, he also tossed his papers onto the pile. These would include his list of the silent auction items he intended to bid on.

Jeff was halfway across the atrium to the doors when he glanced around in time to see the lady approaching the check-in counter. He quickly picked up a newspaper from the nearby stand and wandered over to listen in.

As he neared the area, he heard the clerk ask her name. Her answer was, 'Abigail Chambers.'

The desk clerk joked, "Our town and lighthouse were founded by Sir Michael Chambers. Any relation?"

"That's what I'm here to find out," Abigail whispered with an emotional lump in her throat.

The next day, he discovered that the papers he threw back on the floor included his list of the silent auction items he intended to bid on. When he approached her to get it returned, she not only refused but also made great fun of his paltry amounts.

Again, Jeffrey was furious. He was going to do something about this crazy lady!

Her offenses were too numerous to list. However, they were suspicious and must be researched.

She had numerous papers scattered on the floor of The Sea Crest Inn including her notebook opened to 'Matchmaker' or 'Troublemaker?'

Her arrogant attitude was hard to ignore, no matter how pretty she looked.

She was also unlawfully in possession of his silent auction list of bids for the stay at the Sea Crest Inn and the dinners at The Sea Crest Restaurant.

Attorney Jeffrey Williams was on a mission to get to the bottom of what Abigail Chambers was up to. "Well, I'm also staying at the Sea Crest Inn. Maybe I can ask around and dig up some information on her."

That afternoon, he called his New York City office, "Hello, this is Jeff. I need one of our detectives to run a background check on an individual who just checked into The Sea Crest Inn today."

"Sure, I can put a couple of guys on it that we used for the case of the previous owners of that dog for James Jenson. They tracked down the couple who abandoned the dog in Sea Crest. Maggie found the dog and named it Misha. It would break her heart if anyone came back and took her away, so James went off the deep end and ensured that didn't happen.

"Of course, I remember the detectives. By the way, did you know that Maggie and James got married?"

"You're kidding! Well, what's going on with this guy you want a check on?"

"It's not a guy. It's a young lady, and I use that term loosely. She's going under the name of Abigail Chambers, and that's very suspicious."

"What did she do?"

"Well, I literally ran into her this afternoon. Her belongings went flying all over the floor. I tried to help her pick them up, and she actually yelled at me to leave them alone. She has a terrible temper!"

"Oh no! Well, we can't run a 'check' on everyone with a mean attitude."

"I know that; however, she's a real troublemaker. Her notebooks and papers fell on the floor along with her laptop computer."

"Maybe that's why she was annoyed with you."

"Never mind that. Her notebook was open to 'Matchmaker' or 'Troublemaker'.

"Then, when I followed her to get my stuff back that she'd picked up by mistake, she checked into the Sea Crest Inn. Guess what name she gave them?"

"I have no idea!"

"Abigail Chambers! She said she knows Sir Michael Chambers founded the town and built the Sea Crest Lighthouse, and she plans to find out if she's related."

"Wow!"

"Distant relative of Sir Michael Chambers? I think not!" finished Attorney Jeffrey Williams.

Recipes

For dishes and desserts from

The Masquerade Ball at the Lighthouse

Jumbo Shells *(With Cheese Stuffing)*

Joan Losier

Ingredients:
12 oz Jumbo Shells
1 ½ lbs. cottage cheese or ricotta cheese
8oz. package of mozzarella cheese, finely diced
2 eggs slightly beaten
1/2 tsp. salt
1/8 tsp pepper

1 tsp. chopped parsley
1/4 cup grated Parmesan cheese
3 cups tomato sauce or meat sauce, either canned or homemade

Cooking Instructions:
Cook jumbo shells in 6-8 quarts of rapidly salted water for 12 to 15 minutes. Drain. Combine ricotta and mozzarella cheese with beaten eggs and blend with salt, pepper, and parsley.

Fill the shells with the cheese mixture. Spread a thin layer of sauce in a rectangular baking dish. Place the stuffed shells 1 deep in the baking dish and top with the balance of sauce. Sprinkle with grated cheese and cover with a sheet of aluminum foil. Bake in a moderate oven for 25-30 minutes.

Marinated Chicken

Marc Zacheis

Ingredients:
2 whole chickens (2 1/2 to 3 pounds each), cut in half

For the Basting Sauce:
2 cups cider vinegar
1 cup vegetable oil
1 large egg
3 tablespoons salt
1/2 teaspoon ground black pepper
1 tablespoon poultry seasoning

Cooking Instructions:
Marinate several hours or over-night
BBQ on the grill

Shrimp and Grits

Sandy Wemmerus

Ingredients:
1 lb of shrimp, peeled
6 slices of bacon
1 cup cheddar cheese, shredded
4 tsp lemon juice
1 clove garlic minced
1/2 tsp pepper (optional 3 shakes TABASCO)
1 cup grits
4 cups water
1 tsp salt

Cooking Instructions:
Boil 4 c water. Slowly stir in grits and salt. Reduce heat to med and cook for 5-7 min
Stir in cheese, lemon juice, and pepper
Saute bacon. Remove from pan. Leave 1 Tbs grease
Saute shrimp and garlic for about 3 minutes til shrimp turns pink
Crumble bacon
Add shrimp, crumbled bacon, and grits in casserole
Bake at 350° for 25 minutes

Optional:
Sprinkle the top of the casserole with minced green onions and extra cheese

Seafood Salad

Shannie Hickok and Sally Craig

Ingredients:
1 box of noodles
1 pack of imitation crab (flake style)
1 bag of medium sized cooked shrimp
Bag of peas/carrots
3 cups mayonnaise
Salt and pepper to taste
Old Bay Seasoning to taste
Sugar to taste

Cooking Instructions:
In a bowl, mix the mayonnaise, sugar, salt and pepper, and Old Bay Seasoning to taste
Cook pasta noodles
Add crab, shrimp, and a bag of peas/carrots
Mix everything together in a large bowl
Refrigerate to chill for 2-3 hours or overnight to blend flavors

Spiedies

Marc Zacheis

Ingredients:
1 cup canola oil
2/3 cup cider vinegar
2 tablespoons Worcestershire sauce
1/2 medium onion, finely chopped
1/2 teaspoon salt
1/2 teaspoon sugar
1/2 teaspoon dried basil
1/2 teaspoon dried marjoram
1/2 teaspoon dried rosemary, crushed
2-1/2 pounds boneless lean pork, beef, lamb, venison, chicken or turkey, cut into 1-1/2-to 2-inch cubes

Cooking Instructions:
Marinate meat cubes overnight
Skewer meat like kabobs and cook on BBQ or Grill
Wrap in Italian bread, rolls, or hot dog buns and eat like a sandwich

Turkey Dressing

Vanessa Morris

Ingredients:
Smoked turkey (cut into pieces)
Corn bread, crumbled
Chopped celery
Chopped onion (yellow)
Chopped green onion
Melted butter
Sage seasoning
Poultry seasoning
Salt
Pepper
Onion powder
Garlic powder
Garlic

Grandma Courtright's Special Hot Sauce

Barbara Reed

Ingredients:
30 large tomatoes – or 2 gallons canned
8 large onions
8 hot peppers
8 green peppers
4 cups sugar
3 cups vinegar
4 Tablespoons salt
2 large cans – or – 4 6oz cans of tomato paste

Cooking Instructions:
Peel and chop tomatoes – cook
Chop onions
Take seeds out of peppers and chop
Add all other ingredients to tomatoes
Cook for 4 hours or until thick - on low heat
Stir often as tomatoes will scorch easily
Seal in hot pint or ½ pint jars – Mason or Kerr

Aunt Erma's Chopped Sweet Green Tomato Pickle Relish

Barbara Reed

Erma De La Mater, was my aunt also.
I've been looking for a copy of this recipe for decades.
It's originally from our Grandma Courtright
I'm so glad Barbara had a copy!

Ingredients:
Chop or grind enough green tomatoes to make 1 gallon
Chop or grind 1 large onion
Chop or grind 1 green or red pepper
Stir 1 cup salt in the above mixture & let stand overnight
In the morning, drain & squeeze dry – rinse 2 times & squeeze dry

Add to mixture:
1 tsp mustard seed
1 tsp celery seed
1/2 tsp cinnamon
1/2 tsp cloves
3 or 4 cups sugar

Cooking Instructions:
Cover with vinegar and cook slowly for 1 hour, stir often
Seal in sterilized pint or 1/2 pint jars

Chili

Nancy Jones' Dad

Ingredients:
1&1/2 pounds hamburger
2 cans red kidney beans
2 cans tomato sauce
1 can diced tomatoes
1 small can mild chilies
1 Tablespoon chili powder
1 Tablespoon paprika
1 teaspoon cayenne red pepper
1 teaspoon cumin

Cooking Instructions:
Put in big pot and simmer for 1-2 hours
Serve with homemade cornbread

Green Chili

Ingredients:
1 pound ground beef
1/2 cup chopped onion
1 can (14-1/2 ounces) stewed tomatoes
2 cans (4 ounces each) chopped green chiles
2 cups diced peeled potatoes
2 cups water
1/2 teaspoon salt

Cooking Instructions:
In a Dutch oven or soup kettle, cook ground beef with onion until the beef is no longer pink; drain.
Stir in the tomatoes, green chiles, potatoes, water and salt.
Simmer, uncovered, 45 minutes or until the potatoes are tender.

Corn Relish

Barbara Reed

Her dad's recipe, Linn W. Courtright Jr.

Ingredients:
12-15 Large ears of corn
1/2 cup chopped onion
1/2 cup chopped green pepper
1/2 cup chopped red pepper
1/2 cup chopped celery
1 cup White Vinegar
1 cup water
1 cup sugar
3/4 Tablespoon mustard seed
1/2 Tablespoon salt
1/2 Teaspoon celery seed
1/4 Teaspoon Turmeric

Cooking Instructions:
Blanch corn for 1 minute, cut corn off cob
Mix all vegetables together
Add other ingredients
Cook for 25 minutes
Make a little thickening of corn starch and water
Add to mixture and cook about 5 minutes more
Pack hot in sterilized jars and seal

Grampa Wainwrights Oatmeal Cookies

Barbara Reed

Ingredients:
1/2 cup brown sugar
1/2 cup granulated sugar
1/2 cup shortening
1 egg
1 teaspoon vanilla
1 Tablespoon milk
1 cup flour
1/2 baking soda
1/2 baking powder
1/2 salt
1 cup oats

Cooking Instructions:
Beat sugars, shortening, egg, vanilla and milk together
Sift together flour, baking soda, baking powder and salt
Add to wet mixture
Beat until smooth
Add oats and mix together
Drop by teaspoon on cookie sheet
Bake in preheated 350° oven until done, about 12 minutes

Research and Information

Maritime Heritage Program
Contact the National Maritime Heritage Grant staff at 202-354-6991 or by email: maritime_grants@nps.gov
The United States Lighthouse Society grant - https://uslhs.org/
https://councilofamericanmaritimemuseums.org/
Information on what happened to Chasing the Myth of Confederate Gold
Jefferson Davis fled Richmond with multiple wagons filled with gold and silver. When he was captured, he had almost nothing. Where did the loot go?
https://www.history.com/news/confederate-gold-jefferson-davis
The Legend of the Lost Civil War Gold
httMenups://www.smithsonianmag.com/smart-news/fbi-searching-lost-civil-war-gold-180968581/
Twins: Abbygail and Annabel. These names are becoming very popular again. Scottish and English origin.
Abbygail – 'cause of joy'
Annabel – 'graceful beauty'
'As long as you love me' - Backstreet Boys

About the Author

Carolyn Court is the Pen Name of Carolyn Zacheis. She writes Romantic Suspense novels and has published the first four books in The Sea Crest Lighthouse Series. These novels are present-day stories in which she weaves history and legends from the past. Her love of travel and lighthouses is reflected in her writing. www.CarolynCourtBooks.com

She has visited lighthouses in Asia, Europe, the Caribbean, Bermuda, the USA, Canada, Central and South America, the Galapagos Islands, and Tahiti. She was a longtime member of the Caribbean Tourist Board in Washington, D.C.

For Women's History Month in March, she gave talks and tributes to spotlight and honor the Female Lightkeepers of America.

She is a member of the Lake Authors of the Wilderness and the Faith, Hope, and Love Chapter of The Romance Writers of America. She's also a member of the National Maritime Historical Society, the United States Lighthouse Society, and the Chesapeake Lights Chapter.

Made in the USA
Middletown, DE
21 March 2024